Tribe of Roses

K Stikeleather

Tribe of Roses

KAYLA STIKELEATHER

Dedication

To my daughter, may you always follow your soul and know that you have
a tribe of roses that love and support you.

To Kristopher, my Mateo, who loves me more than I knew how to
imagine.

To Saara, my Soairse, my encouragement & my sister, and her family
who showed me authentic love and support.

To my mom who taught me how to love others deeply and has
sacrificed so much for me.

To my abuela & my aunts who inspire me with their lives & who taught
me how to make tamales in my abuela's kitchen with my mom.

To my Aunt Ranelle who broke barriers by following her dreams.

To all the women in my life who have taught me so much.

To all the Leenas, Eloises, Soairses, Marias, Michelles, Sarahs, every
woman doing their best to heal in a world that is still unbalanced. You
deserve a love without conditions. You deserve more than a Trevor or a
Simon or a Oisin, you are so much more than they could ever let you see.

Acknowledgements

Editor: Kristopher Stikeleather

Trigger Warnings

This book deals with death, grief, depression, abuse, and eating disordered trauma. I am in no way an expert in these topics. The healing journey of the characters in this book, in no way depict professional advice, standards, or methods in which others should replicate. If you or a loved one are experiencing abuse, eating disordered behavior, or depression please seek out a licensed mental health professional.

Taking the first step was hard but finding freedom has been worth the challenge.

Chapter 1

To my future self,

Hey. It's me again. Is it weird that I write letters to myself that I'll never read again? He always told me it was weird. I'm sorry I haven't written in awhile. It's been hard to do anything but just sit in my yellow polka-dot chair in the living room staring at the photo on the wall. Our photo. I remember spending so much time trying to convince him to take that photo. It was a gift for his mom. I bought him a suit and a boutineer. I thought maybe, just maybe if she saw us dressed up, at our best, she could see what I see. She could see how good we are together and how much I love him. How I would give anything to make him happy and how much I would try to be everything he wanted, everything he thought he needed. Instead, she gave it back to us. Said, she didn't need it and that it was a selfish gift anyhow. Maybe she was right.

He never let me take pictures of him after that, so this is the only one I have of us, of him. It's my only visual representation of how he looked. I wish he didn't look so angry in the photo but he was sort of a grumpy man anyhow so I guess it's honest. I'm afraid I'll forget how he looked, how he smelled, how he ate only the corners of french fries, or only dipped his salad in dressing. I'll forget how he only wore black socks and how even though he was a thirty-four year old man, he never learned how to do laundry. I'll forget that he always carried twenty dollars of cash in his wallet and how he never took off his thin gold necklace; not even to shower or sleep.

I heard that's what happens when someone dies, they slowly fade. I'm not ready for him to fade yet. And, part of me, doesn't want the pain to go away, because then he's really gone.

I've never felt so...so....alone, numb to anything but the raging pain of losing him. As I hear the footsteps of the mailman walking past my front door I'm utterly amazed at how the world around me just keeps moving forward while I just...I don't know....slowly suffocate into blackness. It's like my whole body is weighted to this chair. Almost like this piece of furniture and this photo of us have become part of me and moving just feels impossible, unnatural.

My mom came to visit me yesterday. She brought me a journal. Suggested I should write some letters to myself. That it might help. This must be rock bottom because my letter writing to future me has landed me the sacred position of the butt of the family joke since I can remember. But my mom always loved it. She said it was good that I had an outlet. He didn't like it when I wrote and I stopped long before Trevor.

It was nice to see her. It'd been a long time. What....two years? He didn't like my family much. Said they were loud and rude. And Trevor wasn't wrong. I guess in some ways they were. They didn't like him much either and weren't exactly quiet about their feelings of us together. But that doesn't matter now. He's gone. I can't believe he's gone. And now, I'm....I'm alone, again.

I had missed my mom. Her deep brown curls. Her citrus perfume. The way her hugs felt like a deep breath of cold air on a snowy day. Not talking to her was the hardest sacrifice of being with him. I was surprised when I saw her through the door looking glass. Her face was aged more than I remembered and was a little sadder than I had left it. It took all the energy

I had left to get up and get the door. If it weren't for her insistent knocking, I would have been content with my big chair and photo.

I slowly opened the door to let her in.

"Leena," she said as she squeezed me tightly and gave me a kiss on the cheek.

I didn't hug her back. I wanted to but it felt foreign. Like all those years apart created an invisible barrier between us.

"May I come in?" she asked.

I nodded and moved from the entryway. She grabbed a large recyclable bag from the ground full of homemade meals and quickly put them in the refrigerator.

"I made you all your favorites. Mac'n'cheese, lasagna, chicken cordon bleu, tamales, and lots of salad."

I wensed. Salad. I had eaten almost nothing but salad for the last two years and while all the pasta and cheese sounded great, I'm not sure I could allow myself a bite. I shook my head at my mother in acknowledgement and went back to the chair.

"I'm sorry to ask this dear but when is the funeral?"

"Today," I quietly replied. A sharp pain radiated from my chest and lingered in my fingers.

"Today? What time?" she said looking at me confused.

"In about half an hour."

"Oh," she paused looking at me like I had spoken a word she didn't understand. "Are you not going then?"

"I'm not invited. Trevor's mom..," I stopped. His name hurt too much to hear. I took a deep breath and started again. "His mom said I'm just the girlfriend so no need for me to come. They just want family there."

"What?!" My mom's face was starting to turn a light shade of magenta. "That woman! That awful woman. I could just!!! EH!!!" She said every word getting louder as she paced in the kitchen. She stopped and shook her head as if remembering something. She walked over to me and grabbed my hand, "Sweetie, do you want to go?"

Tears began strolling down my stoic face, "It doesn't matter." I wiped my face with the sleeve of my baggie sweater. "I'll be ok."

"So you want to go," she said as a statement instead of a question. "Ok, that's final. We are going!" She walked into my room, opened the closet and pulled out a long black dress. "Look at me." She grabbed my face and stared intently into my eyes. "Always listen to your soul. If your soul is telling you to go, then we must go." She wiped my face with a makeup wipe that she grabbed out of her purse. My mom always carried three things in her purse, makeup wipes, hand sanitizer and red lipstick, her essentials. "Now, here. She handed me the dress." Go put this on. We're leaving in five minutes."

I slowly started to pull off my baggy sweater and matching sweat pants when, for what seemed like the first time, I saw just how small I had become. All I saw was weakness looking back at me in the mirror as I slid on the black maxi dress that had become too baggy for my body. I slowly opened the bathroom door. My mom held in a gasp and came over to me throwing her body on me into a deep hug. "Ok, Leena Marie. You can do this." She said as she put some red lipstick on me and covered my frail arms with her black cardigan. "Let's go."

I climbed into the old red truck that had been in my family longer than me. I had such fond memories of this truck. Getting ice-cream with abuela. Getting picked-up from middle school. Driving it around after homecoming. Heck, one of my brothers even lost his virginity in the truck bed. This vehicle was more part of the family than I was and it felt weird to be riding in it again.

My mom revved the engine as we pulled out of the apartment parking lot. I hadn't been outside in days. My eyes throbbed with pain and my head felt like it was too heavy for my body. As we pulled onto the cemetery road I saw the cars lining the street.

"Just family," my mom said with anger. "That woman! Ok, Sylvia. Calm down. This woman just lost her son. Give her grace," she mumbled to herself as she took her rosary out from the dashboard, kissed it, and did the trinity sign in the air. As we pulled up to the crowded cemetery my mom turned off the engine. It was time and I didn't know what was going to be harder, saying goodbye to him or seeing his mom again.

My mom turned to me, "Ok, sweetie. Are you ready?"

I took a deep breath and looked at my mom. "Thank you mom," I whispered as I climbed out of the truck. Before I could even close the door, she was right beside me holding my hand. "Mom, you don't have to," I said quietly, looking at the ground.

She took me by the chin and held it high. "You have nothing to be ashamed of. You deserve to be here."

I took a deep breath and walked to the funeral ceremony with my mom by my side. I began to get closer, but then I stopped. The truck seemed so far away and his family seemed so close. I looked ahead and began to walk closer and closer until his short, round mother appeared in front of me with a nasty look of hatred in her eyes.

"Hello, Michelle. I'm sorry for your loss," I said quietly, trying to avert contact with her eyes.

"Well, Leena, honestly I'm surprised you're here. I told you on the phone this is just for family."

My mom stood in front of me creating a barrier between Michelle and me. "Hi!" She said with a big grin on her face. She extended her hand towards Michelle. "My name is Slyvie. I'm Leena's mother. It's so nice to finally meet you. And, I am so sorry for your loss. I can't imagine what it's like to lose a child."

Michelle took a step back, not accepting the handshake. "Look, I'm sure Leena is feeling emotional about Trevor's sudden passing, but she really shouldn't be here. It's only family."

"Oh, ok. Well, Leena lived with Trevor for 2 and half years. I'm sure she attended all your family events because she certainly didn't come to ours. So, I think that makes her family. And, even if she isn't, she has every right to be here and get closer just like all your family, which looks to be like the whole town of Summer, Indiana. I see the Berk family, the Snowtown family, oh and is that Betty from the DMV? I didn't know you had such a big family."

Michelle squinted her eyebrows. "Look, I just lost my son and if you won't leave I'll just have to call the police."

"And tell them what? That the girlfriend of the deceased is trespassing on public property? Call them. And I'll call Leena's father. You know, the Sheriff of Greer, the town just outside of Summer so that he can come and work out the details," she replied.

"You wouldn't!" Michelle yelled loudly as pressure began to build in her face.

"Oh, I would. So, you can move now."

Michelle stomped back to the group of people standing around Trevor's coffin.

My mom. This woman. This saint of woman who I didn't deserve was all the strength I needed to stay. As I stood at the front with the immediate family I couldn't believe he was actually gone.

The ceremony was nice. The pastor from his family's church read some scripture and told a funny story about Trevor stealing ice-cream from the church kitchen when he was young. His mom sang a song which was hard to the ears but exactly the type of thing I would have expected her to do. His dad stood in silence like normal. I don't think I've ever heard that man say one word in the three years I dated Trevor. The ceremony ended and I just stood there in front of Trevor's casket. It was lowered by then and partly covered with dirt. I just couldn't believe it. One business trip. One business trip! That's all it took. He left on a Tuesday and never came back. I didn't know my whole life could change so quickly.

"Sweetie, I'm going to pull the truck around now that people are clearing out. I'll give you some privacy. Just come to the truck when you're ready to leave," my mom said as she gave me a hug. I nodded and she left.

As I looked down at what was left of Trevor I couldn't even imagine what life would look like without him. In three years I had changed my whole existence for him. I quit my job. I moved in with him. I stopped hanging out with my friends and family. He made all the decisions and now...now what? I'm not ready for this. I'm not ready for life without him. As I thought about all the ways life was going to be different my throat began to burn and my hands began to shake. My muscles tensed and I began to struggle to breath. I tensed my muscles and released as I exhaled a deep breath. Then suddenly I felt a tapping on my shoulder.

"Hi, you must be Leena." A tall thin woman with a pixie blonde haircut and pink lipstick said smiling. "Are you ok?"

"Hi. No, not really," I replied.

"I am so sorry for your loss. Trevor talked very highly of you."

Confusion covered my face. "I'm sorry, I'm not sure I understand. Who are you?"

"Oh, heavens. Sorry! I'm Sarah. Trevor's friend from college."

He had never mentioned a Sarah. "Oh, of course, nice to meet you," I said confidently, not wanting to hurt this woman's feelings, but definitely not knowing who she was.

"I know this is kind of awkward and I know it's super inappropriate for me to ask but that necklace you're wearing, the gold one," she pointed to my neck.

I put my hand on Trevor's gold necklace that I was wearing. It was mailed to the house with the other belongings found on him after the car crash. "What about it?" I asked.

"Well, Trevor and I...we...we were in love at one point in time and I gave him that necklace."

My heart began to race. I suddenly began to feel like I was trapped in an abandoned elevator buried by rubble and forgotten by the world.

"I was just wondering if I could have it back. It would mean a great deal to me."

I looked at her in shock. I looked at my family's red truck as my mom drove up closer to me and found courage that had been buried for so long. "You're right. That is super inappropriate of you," I said as I walked past the girl and climbed into the truck.

This necklace. This fucking necklace! After three years of dating, Trevor never gave me one single piece of jewelry. In fact, he never gave me a gift at all! Said he didn't believe in them. Was I just his consolation prize because he was my everything!

One year, before I had quit my job, I saved up all my money and bought him this beautiful gold bracelet that matched this fucking necklace and he never once wore it! Never once! And this girl, this woman, gives this necklace to him and he wears it every goddamn day! My internal dialogue was running wild as my heart pounded with anger. I climbed in the truck and slammed the door behind me.

"Honey, are you ok?" my mother said as she drove downtown.

"No."

"Do you want to go home?" she said as she pulled into a Dairy Queen parking lot.

"Not really. I just. I don't know. I just can't be in that apartment....I can't...I can't think straight," I said shaking. I could feel the panic attack coming.

"Sweetie, take a deep breath," she said as she grabbed both of my hands. We took a deep breath together. "I mean your real home. Your brothers have made your room up real nice. You can stay with us for as long as you need. You can even stay forever."

I looked at my mom with tear filled eyes, "I...I...don't know what to say."

"Say, yes," she said, smiling at me. I didn't deserve her. I didn't deserve any of my family. After what I've put them through the last two to three years.

I unbuckled my seatbelt and gave her a big hug.

"Now, do you want to go to the reception dinner at Trevor's parents' house? What is your soul telling you?" she asked, smiling.

"I think my soul has had enough today," I said as I buckled my seatbelt. "Since when did dad become a Sheriff? I thought that took years and the last time I saw him he worked security at the mall."

"Oh, that. He still has the same job. But Michelle doesn't know that. Crazy lady."

And for the first time in a long time I smiled.

Chapter 2

To my future self,

I've been back home now for about a month. The numbness goes away a little bit each day. And then some days it washes over me like new. And, while I know that Trevor wasn't the greatest person, I still really love him even though he's gone. I still can't picture my life without him. And, I still am picking up the shattered pieces of myself he left behind.

I went to our apartment today. My lease ends in a couple of days and Michelle keeps leaving me messages about getting her son's things. She wanted me to make sure I understood that the furniture, bed, kitchen appliances and tv were her sons and so they went back to her and the family. Honestly, she could have it all. I didn't care anymore. I didn't have anything left in me to fight with her. My mom had already cleaned out the refrigerator and packed up most of my things when I moved back home. It was kind of her. She said my soul needed time to heal and I knew she was right.

As my mom and I walked into the apartment I was shocked. It smelled like him. He wore this expensive cologne that costs way more than it should but smelled like it was from the local dollar store. I used to find it a bit overwhelming but now, now I craved it. Most of the stuff in the apartment was gone. "I had your brothers take the furniture and most of

Trevor's things over to his parents' house. I hope that's ok? I'm sorry. I'm realizing now I should have asked. I just wanted her to stop calling you."

"It's ok, mom. Thank you. Really, I appreciate it. And, she has stopped calling, thank you." I wondered why she suddenly stopped leaving me voicemails. Walking through the almost empty house was strange. It's as if our life together had been erased and all that was left was the empty shell I had become.

"The only things that are really left are in your room. Would you like me to help you pack anything?" she asked kindly.

"No, it's ok. I'll be fine." I walked in the room and there it was the polka-dot chair and the photo of Trevor and me. "Mom, why is this chair left?" I wasn't surprised by the photo. The chair was mine. It was something I bought at a thrift store when I first moved in. Trevor hated it but I loved it. He complained for two years about it but I kept it. I'm not sure why, but I'm glad it wasn't gone.

"She said it's ugly and that you can have it," Mom yelled from the kitchen.

"It's mine anyway. I bought it at a thrift store," I yelled back.

"Oh, that makes sense. It looks cool! Kind of funky. Reminds me of when you were in highschool and would thrift for vintage clothes and fix them up."

Wow, that seemed like a lifetime ago, a different person ago.

"You always were a freespirit," she yelled. "It'll look good in your room if you want to keep it."

I didn't feel like a freespirit. That hadn't been me for a long time. I looked at the chair. "I think I'll keep it. But mom?" I asked slowly moving to the kitchen. "Can you get rid of the picture?"

"Are you sure? I thought that was the only photo you had of you and Trevor."

I paused and closed my eyes, "Ya, I'm sure." I didn't want the reminder that I wasn't enough. That maybe I'm still not.

Mom whipped around from the corner, "Ok, sweetie. Hey, you can go home. I just wanted to make sure you had the chance to get anything you might want that's left. Your brothers and I will finish packing and clean the house. Don't worry, we'll make sure you get the deposit back. Your uncles are going to paint and your aunts are bringing over the carpet cleaner. So, go home and don't worry about it. I'll even have your brothers drive you."

I was a little mortified that my entire family knew I was hurting. It felt, I don't know, shameful. But that's typical of my family, we know everything that's going on in each other's lives for better and for worse.

I walked over to the kitchen and found my mom cleaning the stovetop. "The apartment is in Trevor's name. He was just paid-up for a couple of months. He got a special deal if he paid in six month increments."

She dropped her rag and took off her rubber cleaning gloves. "Well, in that case, let's go." She put her arm in mine. "Tony, Alex!" she yelled down the hallway. "Pack it up, we're out of here. And get rid of that photo. She doesn't need it anymore. The uncles will take care of everything else." She smiled at me and whispered, "We will leave this place looking great, not because it's what his family deserves, but because my momma taught me better. Besides, God's wrath is far more just."

I thought about my mom's words. Need it...she doesn't need it anymore. Not, she doesn't want it anymore. Had I needed it? Did I need the reminder of my failures? This photo, the one tangible item that reminded me that we were a couple, even when Trevor was alive. I didn't need it anymore. And that felt somewhat like progress.

Chapter 3

To my future self,

Today was your thirtieth birthday! Can you believe it? I know I can't. I have left my twenties. They are behind me. And, while this should be a very exciting time for me I just feel...I don't know...like I wasted my good years. I had so many dreams and plans and now...I just feel lost. It's like I forgot to know how to dream, to want.

I still miss Trevor and think about him everyday. He wasn't the greatest guy, but we did have some good times. Like the time he planned dinner and bought us my favorite bottle of wine. Or the time where we went to Atlanta for a getaway trip. He just knew me and I knew him. We knew we weren't perfect people, but we chose each other despite our flaws and I guess that's something right?

I've been enjoying being at home. I missed my family and can't believe I gave them up for 2, almost 3 whole years. My younger brother Alex looked like a man now. He even had a mustache. It was a crazy time in the Estrada house. Dad was just promoted to head of security at the mall and passed his interview to get into the police academy in the fall. Tony was just accepted into the airforce and mom was having fun "fattening him up." He was trying to put on muscle which meant he had to eat a lot...I don't know the science. And, I was actually starting to eat again and letting myself enjoy food.

I missed them. I missed family dinners at the table. Making tamales with my aunts and gossiping with my cousins. And I missed food! Trevor was really strict about my diet. He controlled the money and ordered the groceries. I pretty much only ate salad and protein bars. He said it was for my health but he ate cheeseburgers every night.

My mom's mac'n'cheese, my dad's steaks, yum! At first I felt weird eating food other than salads and protein bars. Actually, I got sick. My mom took me to the doctor and she said I was malnutritioned. I self-admitted myself to an eating disorder treatment program for two weeks at the recommendation of my doctor. I also had mandatory therapy in which my therapist explained that Trevor was abusive through food and other things that I'm not ready to write down. Trevor loved me and he wouldn't do anything to intentionally hurt me, right? I just think...I don't know...that he's misunderstood by people who didn't really know him. He just wanted me to be healthy. That's all.

Anyway, it's been about eight months and food doesn't feel so foreign to me anymore. I still get nervous around food and I eat little portions or my stomach aches, but it's been yummy to taste the foods of my childhood; of my culture. Hard but good.

Mom invited the whole family for a big birthday celebration at the house. My uncles even cracked out their guitars. Music, laughter and the smell of good food filled the atmosphere and for the first time in a long time, my heart stopped aching, even if it was only for one night.

I had a huge pile of presents and before I could open any of them my mom and dad made an announcement.

Mom stood up on the self-made wooden stage in our backyard and whistled, getting everyone's attention. "Leena, I love you so much. You are my heart and I cannot tell you how nice it has been having you home," she stopped to wipe her eyes with a hanky my dad handed to her. "Your family, everyone here, is so happy you're back."

My father grabbed my mom by the waist, held her close and took over the speech, "You know, for a moment, I thought I had lost my little girl." My dad, who looks tough but is so tender-hearted, began to wipe his eyes, "Allergies," he said.

The family laughed.

"I am so glad you are home and so proud of you. When you were a girl you used to write these books about a girl named Leena who traveled the world. Remember? You used to use wallpaper samples for the covers. Anyway, I found one of those books the other day when I was cleaning out the garage looking for my guitar for this very party and I thought I would read it if that's ok with you."

I blushed as the whole family looked at me for a moment. I shook my head with consent.

My dad began to read, "Hi, my name is Leena Estrada. I have two brothers who like to draw and paint. One day they are going to be famous. But not me. I don't want to be famous, I just want to travel and write. Here is where I'll go."

The family awed.

"I will go to the North Pole and finally prove Santa is real."

Laughter filled the party.

"I will go to Finland and pet the reindeer. I will go to France and eat stinky cheese. And I will go to Ireland to learn to play music with my dad who is obsessed with Irish melodies. The end."

The party erupted in applause and whistles.

"As all of you know, Leena actually went to Ireland for her summer study abroad where she studied Literature. She loved it so much that she came back and told us she wanted to move there one day and let me tell you that broke our hearts. We were so excited that she found her passion but so worried she would move away and we would hardly see her," dad said as he began to cry again, slurring his speech.

My mom took over, "Leena, we love you so much and after everything you've been through we wanted to help support your passion in ways we regret not doing before. So, we have purchased airline tickets to Ireland. You leave for Galway in two weeks if you want to go. We rented you a small apartment and it's within walking distance to the university. It's all paid for. And we have tickets to come see you in a month. And you can move back anytime no questions asked. I never will not support your dreams again, Leena. Never."

My father looked at me and smiled, "It was destiny that you wrote this book. It was destiny that I found it. And now when you've lost so much, it's destiny to return to the place that gave you your passion. Follow your soul because when you do, serendipity becomes your normal. After all, it's the universe's way of telling you, you are on the right path."

My eyes began to well. I completely forgot about Ireland. I forgot about writing. I forgot about everything I loved. I gave it up for Trevor and I thought he was enough. Or maybe I didn't think I was enough. But this yearning to go, even though I was terrified, was suddenly welling up in my heart, like it had been there all along just waiting to be unleashed. Like something was being uncovered, I just don't know what that something was. I could feel my hands trembling. I shook my head yes and ran to my parents hugging them tightly. "Thank you," I whispered.

My mom cupped my face and looked deeply into my eyes, "Go eat potatoes and drink beer. Go have an adventure. Your soul will guide you."

I shook my head and hugged them tight.

Chapter 4

To my future self,

Ireland is just as beautiful as you remembered it. As you walked the cobble roads of Galway it's as if you were welcomed by a close friend you hadn't seen in years. The city was pretty much the same. The same vendor that sold you your favorite floral headband is still working at the market. Her name is Eloise and she's invited you for coffee next week.

It was strange being back in Galway. It was everything I remembered and hoped would be. The sounds of woodwinds and singing filled the streets with wonder and excitement. The tiny pubs reminded me that it's ok to just have a few close friends instead of a lot of acquaintances you don't know well. I'm still trying to figure out public transport. Growing up in the rural midwest may have been my downfall in that area.

I have a little one bedroom apartment in Eyre Square. It's humble but enough, and with the location, must be costing my parents a fortune. The whole family must have pitched in. I've never been one to ask for help or receive it, but I'm glad I came. Having a different environment just feels...I don't know...like it's just what I didn't know I needed.

I still miss Trevor and think about him everyday, but not every second. Everywhere I look my eyes search for him. Hoping he'll just appear like nothing ever happened. When I'm sleeping I feel his body wrapped around mine and wake up to an empty bed. And everytime I search for him or feel weighted by him in bed my body panics. I freeze and my hands begin to throb. I take a deep breath, close my eyes, tighten all my muscles and relax. And the panic slowly fades. I wonder if things will always be this way. If my heart will always miss him. And, someday, I wonder if I'll ever truly be in love again. I'm not sure I want that. I just want to feel like me again, but I'm not sure what being me really feels like.

Oh, I almost forgot to mention, I was accepted at National University of Ireland, Galway. I begin in a couple of months. I'll be starting a Master's of Writing. I have no idea what I'll do with it...but I'm letting my soul have what it wants and this feels right. It's only a year long which is good because I've already spent enough time away from my mom. Anyway, everything is just working out which has to be a sign I'm making the right choices...right? I applied for a scholarship that covers most of my tuition and my federal loans will cover everything else. I'm even moving into an on-campus apartment with a roommate the school is going to match me with. That's a bit nerve racking. I've never lived with a roommate I didn't know. Even in undergrad I had an apartment with my boyfriend Simon.

Don't get me wrong, I love my apartment! It's in the perfect location, but I know it has to be costing my family so much and I don't want to be a burden. I've already done enough to them over the last couple of years and I know they mean well, but I just can't keep taking their money. It's been so long since I've made decisions for myself. It feels a bit foriegn. The past couple of weeks have been terrifying but everytime I make a choice I feel lighter. It's like my confidence is slowly being pieced back together. What to eat, where to live, to go back to school; I needed to make these choices for myself and I'm doing it. It's hard but I'm doing it.

This morning I looked at myself in the mirror and was reminded that I'm still healing. Although I'd filled out a bit, my cheeks were still hollow and the bags around my eyes were still dark. As I clenched Trevor's gold necklace that dangled from around my neck I felt guilty. Guilty that I was alive and he was gone. Guilty that for a moment I felt happy when he couldn't feel anything. I know it sounds crazy, but I'm not sure I can move on. I'm trying. I really am, but a big part of me doesn't want to grow. Part of me wants to stay still in my sadness and just hurt.

Eating has gotten better. I have a new doctor here in Ireland that takes my vitals every Tuesday at noon and my doctor from home checks in with me once a month along with the twice a month therapy sessions with Dr. Gillion. She's been great, but I'm just not sure I'm ready to open up again.

Chapter 5

To my future self,

So much has happened. I'm not sure where to start. I went for coffee with Eloise and she actually offered me a job, which was nice because I started to slip back into numbness. A deep wave of grief just hit me one day. It took everything in me to get out of bed to meet up with her and honestly if I didn't have the plans, and if Eloise wasn't the cutest, sweetest little old lady I had ever met, I would have probably stayed in bed for who knows how long.

We met at this cute little coffee shop called Pascal Coffee House. The white walls, dark brown wood furniture, and black and white photos that hung on the walls reminded me of a little coffee shop I went to in New York City on my high school senior trip. Simon had to go there because some famous influencer owned the place and would show up occasionally. This place was different though. Beautiful flowers laid on every table in delicate white porcelain pitchers. It smelled of chocolate crepes and dark roasted coffee. It was enchanting and just the place I would think Eloise would pick.

She ordered us an afternoon tea box that was filled with scones, fruit, pancakes, jams, and sweet dips. While I mentally calculated the calories Eloise put her hand on mine and my internal critic was silenced. She had this unexplainable calming effect on me. I didn't eat much but more than I would have otherwise. I wasn't past the habit of not enjoying my food yet.

We talked about her shop and how she got started. She has the most beautiful love story. She grew up in Indiana which was shocking to me! I assumed she was American or Canadian from her accent but I never would have thought we would have grown up in the same state? Anyway, she grew up in Muncie, Indiana which isn't too far from where I grew up.

She went to college at Purdue University, a public school in Lafayette and won a scholarship to study abroad in Ireland. It was only a summer study abroad, but she never left. She came and fell in love with Gallaway and never went back.

"I find the city here intoxicating and I found a real community here in Galway," she explained.

I nodded my head smiling.

"You know, I met a boy and decided to stay. He was a local. Worked at a local pub at the time. He walked me home one night and asked me to dance on the cobblestones. I was his before I knew what happened."

A pain shot out from deep within my heart and radiated through my fingers. I began to feel the water in my eyes well up. She put her soft aged hand on top of mine once again and warmth radiated through my body. I wasn't sure what hurt more; being reminded that I used to love someone like that, or knowing that my love story was so shallow compared to hers.

"What's wrong dear? Did I say something to offend?" she questioned with a look of deep care in her eyes.

"No, no it's not that. I'm sorry, it's nothing," I said as I drank a gulp of water trying to shock my body into normalcy.

"Do you want to talk about it?"

"I...I lost my boyfriend, Trevor, almost a year ago. I'm still...I don't know," I said, shaking my head looking down at the table.

"Loss is a hard thing. I lost my Cian about ten years ago. Life hasn't been the same without him."

"I'm sorry," I whispered looking deep into her yellow stained brown eyes.

She squeezed my hand, "Oh, it's alright. He was a good man. I almost lost myself in him once. Tried to be everything he needed me to be without realizing I needed me too. He sat me down one day and said, 'El, I love you, but I miss the you that would dance with me on the old cobble road in the middle of the city. The girl that swept me off my feet.' At first, I was really upset with him. I mean, how dare he after everything I did for him, everything I became for him. The child I had bore for us. But then I realized I was lucky. Lucky, I had a partner that cared so deeply about me that he would risk having me to make sure I was who I wanted to be and not what I thought he wanted me to be. I'm sure he was nervous when I left."

"You left him?" I said in shock.

"Of course. I needed to be my own woman again and to do that I needed a change. My parents took the baby and I left. I told them I would be back in two weeks and left Cian a note saying the baby was with my parents for a couple of weeks and that I didn't want to see him again. I was very upset, you know."

I shook my head as I leaned in with interest.

She took a sip of her coffee, "That is good coffee," she patted her lips dry with a napkin and placed it back on her lap. "I signed up for one of those bus tours. You know the ones the tourists take. I packed a little red backpack and off I went. And when I was gone I met a man. His name was Peter. He had just divorced his wife and needed a change of scenery. We had a little love affair those two weeks but he wasn't Cian. I came back changed...and pregnant."

My eyes widened, "And Cian took you back?"

"Yes, and he raised our son Aidan not really ever knowing if he was his biological father."

"Wow," I said as I looked down at my coffee. "He really cared about you."

"Wow, indeed. One night Peter and I were laying in the grass looking at the stars and I had surprised him with these chocolate scones I had bought at the last stop. But when I gave them to him he made some little comment about how I shouldn't eat this late at night, jabbing at my weight. That's when the facade started to melt. I was so hurt by Cian that I got swept up in a romance with a man who didn't want me, he just wanted someone to control or a fling and I was not going to be that woman. It's not what I wanted. I had already changed once for one man and I wasn't going to do it again for another man. What I really wanted was Cain, and I'd hope I wasn't too late and hoped I hadn't hurt him too much. I left Peter that night. Slipped out while he fell asleep and never saw him again. Instead I hiked the Black Mountain Ridge Trail and headed home to Cian."

"Was he mad about Peter?"

"Of course. Well, I'm not sure mad is the right word. He was hurt and I was hurt that I hurt him. Men like Peter break you down slowly so you become normalized to their brutality. They give little warning signs you learn to ignore. But men like Cain; they are patient, kind, they don't use pride to hurt you, they have reasonable boundaries. I had never met a man like that before I met Cain. I always tried to be someone who deserved him. But I learned something very important during that trip. I was enough, even if I didn't believe it and even if no one had ever told me that before Cain. He forgave me. We went to counseling which was very counterculture for him and for the time, and we healed. We even had a marriage renewal ceremony. He said I looked stunning in my white dress, even though I was eight months pregnant at the time. And that was that. We were inseparable until his death. I still think he lingers around, watching over me and bringing the right people to me at the right time," she smiled and looked at me as she sipped from her coffee.

I smiled back. "That's beautiful."

"Only, because it's true. And what about you? How did you meet Trevor?"

"A dating app," I replied a little embarrassed.

"How modern," Eloise smiled.

"Well, I had just gotten out of a long relationship with my college sweetheart Simon and I wasn't exactly looking for something long-term, but Trevor was very charismatic."

"A charmer was he?"

"Very much so. He just said all the right things and the sex..was so.." I closed my mouth suddenly.

"Oh, it's ok. I might be old but I'm not a prude. So the sex was good," she said as she took a bite of her scone.

I let out a laugh and nodded, "He just felt new in a way I hadn't experienced. I knew Simon since grade school and we stayed together all throughout college. Simon had just broken things off about a month before I met Trevor. He was just so kind to me and so generous. But then he...I don't know...changed."

"Hmm...how so?" she questioned politely.

"He started to make little comments and..."

"He was a Peter wasn't he?" she questioned curtly.

"Maybe...I just...eventually...I just...I don't know...lost myself in him, or maybe in his expectations and his family hated me."

"What heavens for? You seem like a delight."

"I don't know. I think they just pictured someone different for him."

"Someone a little more vanilla," she looked me up and down. "I grew up near that town. I know."

"Honestly, maybe or maybe not. I'm not sure. He had a weirdly close relationship with his mom so maybe it was just that, but the whole family...I just...they never....I always felt like a square trying to fit into the circle of their family. I tried to change, I did everything they asked but....it just was never enough. I was never enough," I looked down at the table trying to fight back tears.

Eloise grabbed my hand once more, sending a stream of warmth through my body, "Honey, you're not a square or a circle. You're a rose."

We sat and talked for what felt like forever. A week later I was working in her shop that she opened during the winter when the city market closed. I worked alongside her selling old books, scarves, and flowers. I know, quite an interesting mix. I asked Eloise about her shop one day and she said she only sells things she loves. It's her way of sharing herself with others. But I think maybe it's her way of reminding herself of who she is.

Chapter 6

To my future self,

The past couple of weeks haven't been easy. Don't get me wrong, working in Eloise's shop has been the only thing getting me out of bed in the morning. People watching through the small window in her shop and modeling new scarf designs for Eloise has been the only thing keeping me going. I didn't know my heart could hurt this bad. Trevor wasn't just my boyfriend, he became my whole life and trying to rebuild what vanished in an instant was terrifying and hard.

It's like everytime I take a step forward and start to let some of the pain go I just feel guilty and overwhelmed with grief. I'm just not sure my heart wants to be happy, or maybe it's just been so long it doesn't know what happiness is anymore.

The new year was just another day for me. Eloise invited me to her son's family house in the country, but I just couldn't get myself out of bed. Every year around this time I went to Trevor's family's house. They had a bbq and pool party. I remember those events being oddly quiet. Like everyone was tiptoeing trying not to draw attention to themselves. I never swam. I don't even think I spoke. I didn't want prying eyes on my body or my mind. They had enough material to criticize. I didn't need to give them more. Trevor would always serve my plate. A small salad and one rib. He let me splurge on holidays. I would even drink a glass of champagne which would leave me light headed and ready to go home.

My parents were supposed to come for the holidays, but something came up. They wouldn't tell me exactly what was going on. I assume the money just didn't work out. They lived a humble but full life and money wasn't something that was always readily available. I'm not too concerned though, my aunts would have let me know if there was anything to worry about. But I felt the absence of my mom. I lost her for so long and getting her back, my best friend, filled an emptiness that Trevor could never fill. She called me once a day via video chat. But lately I have been missing her. For about two weeks she's called with the video function turned off. When I ask her if everything is ok she says, "Of course, sweetie! I just don't know how to use this new phone your brother got for me. That's all." My brother just landed his first real job. He saved up his paychecks for a whole month to buy my mom that phone and he wouldn't take no for an answer when he gave it to her. If I had any money left I would have hopped on a plane and had a proper Christmas with my big loud family. I missed them and my longing for them mixed with my grief from Trevor was hard, but I was looking forward to school and writing again.

I move into my apartment next week. My roommate is a local girl. Her name is Saoirse. I met her for coffee the other day at this trendy coffee shop called Esquires Coffee, here in the square. They only sell organic fair trade coffee and they have an industrial but warm feel with the unique floor tiles which I assume are hand painted shades of brown, industrial lighting, subway tile backsplash, and rustic repurposed wood used as accents throughout. It was very modern, yet warm which can be hard to pull off with a contemporary design. Or so I think, I took a couple of interior design courses in high school. My dream was to become an architect, or so I thought. What I really wanted I wouldn't let myself have;

to become a writer. I just, I don't know, never thought I was good enough or maybe I was just too scared to really share, open up, be authentic in my stories. It doesn't matter now, I'm giving it a go. If Trevor's death has taught me anything it's that I can't just keep waiting for my life to change, I'm worthy enough to try.

Saoirse said the coffee shop is her favorite place to grab a coffee on her daily walk through the square. She loves it because it's still a little underrated so the lines aren't too long. However, I think her affinity is really for the beautiful Spanish barista. She leaned over and gave him a kiss on the cheek when she picked up her coffee. When I asked her if she was dating him she told me she doesn't date but they had hooked up a couple of times. I've never been bold enough to do anything like that and while my upbring tells me to look down on her, all I feel is admiration in her confidence.

Saoirse is a bit wild in her own way. Her bright curly red hair, deep blue eyes, and porcelain freckled skin was noticed everywhere she went. She wore the most beautiful unique clothes which she made by hand as to not support industries that contributed to global warming. Her matter-of-fact curtness was a bit off-putting but I loved that she knew exactly who she was and was unapologetically herself.

I must have seemed like a mouse compared to Saoirse, but she was kind and adventurous and I think she is exactly who my roommate is supposed to be. I'm terrified to be living with another person, especially in my condition as of late but she reminds me of the girl I used to be, or pretended to be, instead of the woman I've become.

"So, you're American?" she said as she sat down to a small empty table by a glass window at the entrance.

"Yes," I sipped my chai soy tea latte. My hands began to shake, she was a bit intimidating and I was nervous.

She looked me up and down. I couldn't help but wonder if maybe she was disappointed in me, that little me was her roommate, "So, what are ya?"

"What do you mean?" I replied.

"Everytime I meet an American they say, 'their half this and a quarter that and blah blah blah.' So have it out will ya? I know you're dying to tell me." She rolled her eyes and took a big bite of a chocolate chip cookie which oozed all over her mouth. She had no remorse as she continued to eat her cookie.

I smiled, "Well, I'm a quarter Mexican but mostly Irish."

"Oh, so you're one of those Americans that thinks they're Irish, are ya?" she looked at me as she sipped on her cup of black coffee, having finished her cookie.

"No, I've always identified more with my Mexican culture. My father was Irish, his family migrated over in the 60's. But he left when I was 8 and my dad, technically my stepdad is Mexican and has a big family, so his family and my mom's Mexican/Spanish family get together for big events and I don't know, I just don't know much about my Irish culture."

"So that's why you're here then?" she questioned.

"No, not really. I actually came here by chance years ago. I was signed up for a study abroad trip to Turkey but not enough people signed up for the trip, so I had the option to go to Ireland or Asia, and I thought Ireland fit more with my program of study."

"Or you subconsciously came here to learn more about your father?" she looked at me assuredly.

"Maybe. Ok, well what about you. What's your story?" I asked.

"Well, I have a degree in Environmental Studies and did a short course in New York City studying fashion. My goal is to revolutionize the fashion industry with stylish designs that use green materials. It's my thesis for the fashion master's degree."

"That's really cool! I used to love shopping at thrift stores and fixing up the clothes," I said smiling. She was kind of inspiring.

"Used to?"

"Ya, I don't really do that anymore. It's been a long time."

"Shame. Enough about me. So you came here as part of a study abroad, then what happened?"

"Well, I fell in love with Ireland. It's just so beautiful here and I love the people and the culture. I really wanted to move here long-term but my family wasn't super supportive so I stayed and my longtime boyfriend at the time moved here and we broke things off."

"And you guys are back together now?"

"Oh, no. I don't even know if he's still here."

"We should definitely call him. See if he wants to get drinks later."

"No, that's ok."

"Come on. Be adventurous. You are in Ireland, right?"

"Ok, what the hell," I pulled out my phone. I couldn't believe I was doing this. What was his number....?? 869- no 968-. Ah, that's it! 968-343--I dialed the rest of the numbers. The phone began to ring.

"Hello?" A deep familiar voice asked.

Shock traveled through my body. What had I done? What am I doing? "Uh, Simon?" I embarrassingly sputtered.

"This is Simon," he responded.

Oh, no. He doesn't even remember my voice. "Ok, bye," I said as I clicked the phone off.

"You chicken!" Saoirse yelled as she redialed the number from my phone log. "Tell him to meet us at The Kings Head at 10, there's a band playing there tonight," she threw the phone at me as it started to ring.

"Hello? Hello?" Simon's voice echoed through the phone.

"Simon? Are you there?" I questioned.

"Who is this? How did you get this number?" he asked.

"You really don't remember my voice?" I replied. Saoirse was giving me the thumbs up from across the table.

There was silence on the other end. I thought maybe he had hung up but in a soft tone he said, "Leena? Is that really you?"

"Ya, I'm in Galway!" I said quickly.

"Wow, I live in a small town near there. Do you want to get together soon? Maybe catch up? I know of a great place where we could catch dinner nearby."

"Well, my roommate and I are going to The Kings Head around 10 tonight, there is a band playing tonight. Want to meet up with us?" I replied.

There was a long pause.

Saoirse looked at me confused.

"Hello? Simon, are you there?" I asked.

"Ya, I'm here. Look Leena, I want to be honest with you. I really want to see you but I'm married now and I have a 6 month old baby boy so I don't really go out to the pubs anymore. At least not the way I used to."

"Oh, wow, that's great, good for you. I ah, I have to go."

"Leena?"

"I have to go but I'll see you soon, maybe. I'll ah, I'll give you a call," I quickly hung up the phone.

"That was awkward," Saoirse said.

My face felt like it was burning. "Why did I do that?" I whispered under my breath. I'm an idiot. Of course he moved on. Of course he's married with a kid. He deserved that. For so long I thought that's what we would have but that's not going to happen now. What did I do? Why wasn't I enough?

"Are you ok? What's the big deal?" Saoirse grabbed another cookie from her bag and took a big bite. "It's just a boy. You're young and smart, there are more boys. Or girls. Whatever you're into."

I grabbed my purse from the ground and looked up at Saoirse who was finishing her coffee. "I have to get to work, but I'll see you next week on move-in day?"

"You don't want to check out the band at The Kings Head?" she questioned, confused.

"Oh, ah...maybe."

"I'll take that as a firm yes. I'll see you tonight at 10," she wrapped the rest of her cookie, put it in her purse and grabbed her black shiny jacket from the floor. "Hey, I'm sorry about Simon, but at least now you know. And if you want romance, I know a lot of great guys who would die for a date with a girl like you. I mean you're great, what's not to like?"

I smiled. She must see something in me I can't. Maybe I will go? "So, what should I wear tonight?" I asked.

Saoirse locked arms and said, "Do you have time for shopping? Or do you really have to get to work?"

"I have an hour or so."

"Oh, I thought the work thing was just a way to get out of coffee," she said confused.

I smiled and together we walked out of the coffee shop and down the cobble road.

Chapter 7

To my future self,

Yesterday was filled with the unexpected. Saoirse was a force of nature, much like my mom. I envisioned she was much like Saoirse when she was younger. She was inspiring with her boldness and creativity. Honestly, I was a bit intimidated by her but in a way that made me want to be better. If that makes sense?

We had a great afternoon of shopping. She took me to this hidden thrift store and made me swear not to tell a soul where it was. There were rows of colorful and forgotten items each with its own story. Saoirse said every piece of clothing is the perfect item if it's styled right. I'm not sure if I agreed but I loved her passion for making others feel empowered through clothing.

She styled me in this tight maroon red dress that puffed at the sleeves and buttoned down the back. I told her all about the writing program and how I was really excited about my classes. We tried on so many beautiful and weird clothes. It was refreshing. When I showed the maroon dress to Eloise she gasped saying it was the most beautiful dress she'd ever seen. She even gave me this beautiful black scarf to put in my hair that went perfectly with the dress.

After work I practically ran to my apartment. I locked the door, ran past the window and straight into my bathroom. For the first time in a long time I did my make up. Natural creamy foundation, a light bronzer to highlight my cheekbones, a little bit of deep red blush on my round cheeks, dark smokey eyes, and a deep red lip. I squeezed into my dress, slid on the heels Saoirse insisted I buy, they were only two euros, and tied the black scarf in my hair. My heart began to race as I walked closer to the mirror. As I looked at the reflection a shiver ran down my back. I didn't recognize the reflection staring back at me. Was this me? For the first time in a long time, I felt beautiful. It wasn't the makeup, it wasn't the dress, I saw me, not who I used to be but who I will one day become, confident.

I met Saoirse at the pub and she was stunning as usual. I mean I assume it was normal...I had only just met her hours before but somehow I felt like we had been friends for years.

"Hi, Leena! Over here!" she yelled as she waved her hand trying to get my attention.

I walked over to her trying not to fall in my heels. It had been a long time since I wore shoes like this and I was a bit wobbly. "Hi, Saoirse! You look beautiful!"

"Thanks! And you are certainly wearing that dress! It looks just right. You will surely win Simon's heart." she said as she puffed on her e-cigarette and batted her long red eyelashes.

"Oh, no. That's not what...he's married...I..." In all the fun of today I completely forgot that I had invited Simon out tonight. But he did say this wasn't his scene and that he's married. Married. It sounds so...so grown up. We had always talked about getting married and having a big family and now he has begun that dream, but without me. A pain shot up my chest and lingered in my hands. "He's not coming, and anyhow, he's married so he's moved on and it's ok, I mean I moved on, I..." Trevor. My eyes began to well with tears. I stood still in silence.

"What's going on here?" Saoirse said as she waved her e-cig up and down motioning at my face.

"Nothing," I said as I cleared my throat and took a deep breath.

And like my mom, she grabbed my face, looked me in the eye and said, "I don't know what's going on, or what happened, but he asked to meet up with you. Happily married men don't do that. He'll show. You're too beautiful in every way for him not to. But listen, Leena. It's your choice what happens next and you don't have to choose him. Hell, you don't have to choose anyone but yourself. Fuck men! And fuck, Simon! It doesn't matter what happened, he let you go. And now you have the choice what's next. So what do you say?"

I looked down at my ridiculously high heel shoes and thought what would my mom do. "I say, we drink!"

Saoirse smiled and grabbed my hand as we ran into the pub that was blaring with the music of a local band composed of a cello, a violin, a fiddle, drums, and a male singer. My body vibrated as the speakers blasted the woodwind sounds. The pub was packed. Saoirse grabbed my hand tight as we squeezed through the crowd to the bar. Saoirse said something to the bartender and he slid me a beer.

I smiled at the bartender in acknowledgement. "What did you say to him?" I asked Saoirse.

"Just that he ought to buy us a beer of course," she smiled and we both laughed. "Do you want to venture to the front?"

"Sure!" I mean I was already here. Why not embrace the full experience, right? When in Ireland, right?

She grabbed my hand and together we fought our way to the front much to the disapproval of the girls now standing behind us. Although I didn't know a word of the music Saoirse knew every line. We danced and jumped and took our heels off. Our feet sticking with every jump against the dirty pub floor.

After what seemed to be an hour the band paused. The lead singer, who made my heart thump with his shoulder length red brown hair and hazel eyes looked directly at Saoirse. "Well, if it isn't my friend Saoirse. I think I need someone to come up and help me sing the next song," he said into the mic.

She knew him? Of course she did, all attractive people know each other, right?

Saoirse jumped up and took the mic, "Now dear brother."

Brother? Oh, no! Was it weird I thought her brother was attractive? Awkward, right?

"I'm not sure I'm up to it tonight," Saoirse replied, "You see I'm losing my voice because I sang every word with you, but I have a dear new friend here tonight and I think she would be perfect to be your backup. Welcome Leena from America who is Mexican and Irish!"

I rolled my eyes at Saoirse who was still teasing me about the American heritage thing, "No, I'm not doing it," I replied as I crossed my arms.

"Come on Leena, you know you want to," the lead singer taunted as Saoirse shook her head in agreement.

How could I say no to him? Saoirse's brother! I reminded myself. "I don't even know the song?" I replied.

"Ok, well you can pick the song. What would you like to perform?" he asked.

I thought for a second and then it came to me, my go-to karaoke song from my early college days. I climbed up on stage taking Saoirse's hand as leverage. I walked over to the lead singer and grabbed his face and brought it in real close. I could feel the jealous eyes of girls in the crowd looking at me in envy. I pretended to go in for a kiss but instead whispered the song in his ear.

Saoirse looked at the crowd, pointed a thumbs up at me and winked as she mouthed, "This girl," to the crowd.

"Ladies and Gentlemen Leena Estrada singing Toxic by Brittany Spears!" her brother announced. The crowd cheered.

"You have got to be kidding me, Leena," Saoirse said as she rolled her eyes.

I smiled in victory. "The taste of your lips I'm on a ride," I sang as I danced and pointed to people in the crowd. The people watching joined in singing the retro song from their parents' childhood. As the song came to an end the crowd erupted in applause and whistles.

The lead singer grabbed my hand and raised it high, "Leena, everyone!" I climbed down the stage and headed to the bar for a much needed glass of water. My head felt dizzy with adrenaline but my throat burned with strain, feeling as though I had been walking in a desert with no water for weeks.

The bartender graciously handed me a glass of water. As I gulped it down I felt a tap on my shoulder.

"Still jamming out to Brittney Spears, are ya?"

Simon? I quickly turned around. "Simon, is that you?"

He smiled while he wrapped his arms around me. "It's great to see you Leena."

"You too, Simon. It's been a long time."

"Hey do you want to get out of here?" he asked as he let me go.

I nodded my head yes. I gestured to Saoirse letting her know I was heading out. The lead singer gave me a frown. "Bye Leena, we'll have to meet again," he said over the mic as I walked out of the pub with Simon.

As we exited The Kings Head a shiver ran down my body. It had dropped about 10 degrees and the short bodycon dress with no shoes was not keeping me warm. Simon took off his jacket and wrapped it around me. He always was a gentleman. I'm glad that hasn't changed. But he did seem different, tired. But I guess having a baby will do that.

We walked over to a stone ledge and sat. The cold rock was jolting but Simon's smile kept me warm.

"So, you came?" I stated.

"Well, you hung up so quickly. I thought this might be the only opportunity I would have to see you," Simon fell silent creating distance between us.

"I, uhm, got a scholarship to study writing at NU. I start soon."

"That's great Leena," he was looking down at his shoes. A wave of sadness seemed to wash over him. His body slumped and lay in the middle of it.

"Can I ask you a question without it sounding rude?" he said, still looking at the ground.

"Sure. I guess," that was an odd thing to ask, I thought to myself.

"Why are you here?" he questioned. "Why are you really here?"

"What do you mean? I'm here studying writing."

"I know you better. You love it but...nevermind," Simon fell silent again then looked me straight in the eye. "If you're here for me you're too late. I have a baby girl now."

"Simon, I didn't come for you. And if you knew I loved writing, why did you make me feel like an idiot every time I wrote."

"I didn't do that!" he exploded.

"Yes, you did," I stated, holding my ground and my truth.

"Leena, you can't honestly think that."

"Stop. Just stop. I'm not crazy, Simon. And it doesn't matter anymore because we're not together," I reminded him.

"I waited for you, Leena. I waited for you to come around. I tried to move on and I couldn't. You were my everything, Leena. You still...it's too late now."

"What are you talking about? You broke up with me," I reminded him.

"Because you wouldn't move to Ireland and now you're here. It seems a bit odd, don't you think?"

"That's super egotistical, Simon. I'm really not here for you. I can be in the same place as you and not be here for you. I loved Ireland, you knew that. And GU has an incredible writing program."

"So, it was me. I wasn't enough," he replied getting angrier.

"No, Simon, I wasn't enough, because you broke up with me. You chose Ireland. You didn't choose me. So, what was it Simon? What part of me wasn't worth it?"

"I...I can't believe you're turning this around on me."

I took a deep breath. "Whatever, Simon. I think it's time for me to go."

"My Angie, she's great, you know. She's kind and generous and makes me want to be a better man," he replied.

"I'm happy for you. Really."

"I don't want you to be happy for me. I want you to fight for me. You never fought for me!" His voice began to shake, "You know, I came back about a year and half ago and you were nowhere to be found. I called your work, you quit. I asked your family, they said they didn't know how to reach you. I went to all your favorite places and you were nowhere to be found. I looked for you for weeks. And to this day I still look for you whenever I'm in public. Do you know what that feels like? You did that to me Leena and I don't even care because..."

"Say it," I needed to hear it.

Simon looked at me in confusion. "Because I love you, Leena. I always have since we were kids. You were supposed to be my happily ever after. We were supposed to have the fairytale ending."

"Maybe, but you didn't choose me and now it's too late. You choose the people you love. You love the idea of us but you don't love me."

"That's not fair."

"No, it's not. I loved you so much, but you hurt me so deeply that I didn't know if I would ever recover and now...now someone has broken me into someone I don't even recognize. I'm not that Leena anymore, she left a long time ago. She's gone."

"What do you even mean? You seemed fine tonight singing and dancing and flirting with that guy!" he pointed to the pub as he screamed, his hostility growing.

And in that moment something came over me. I remember what Saoirse said, 'It's your choice what happens next.' "Fuck you, Simon," I whispered.

"What did you just say to me?" he questioned in shock. His Leena would never speak to him that way or any person for that matter.

I stood up and looked directly at him, "Fuck you!" I screamed. "You broke up with me! You broke my heart, and why? Because I wouldn't move here for you! And now you are married with a child and you are mad at me for having fun tonight. I'm single, I can flirt with whomever I want. You're the one who is married. Why are you here?" I started to pace in front of him. "The first night of fun I had in the past 2 and half years because I lived with some narcissistic controlling man who managed every aspect of my life including what I could and couldn't eat, and for one night I had a moment of release and you are here criticizing me. Go home to your wife, Simon. We're done here," I threw his coat at him and walked away shaking partly from the adrenaline and partly because it was still freezing outside. But, you know what? I didn't care. For the first time, I felt free.

Saoirse came over and linked arms with me, "Ya, fuck you, Simon!" she screamed as we walked away. "Don't worry, love. I've got you," she said as we walked confidently barefoot down the cobble road, her brother behind us carrying our shoes.

I think I like this Saoirse. She might just turn out to be the truest friend I've ever had.

Chapter 8

To my future self,

I didn't want to get out of bed this morning. I was still in my dress from last night. My makeup was smeared half on my pillow and what remained of my lipstick was somehow all over my chin. After a few drinks with Saoirse after my episode with Simon, I somehow ended up back in my room.

If it weren't for the smell of pancakes and coffee I probably wouldn't have woken up. As I stumbled out of my room and into the living room a man in the hot pink apron my mom sent me came out with two mugs filled with some sort of liquid.

I screamed in shock. "Who are you and why are you in my apartment?" I questioned.

"Ah, quieter Leena. I have a massive hangover," Saoirse said in a groggy voice.

"Oh, you look familiar, who are you again?" I asked the strange man who I assume Saoirse knows as I tried to piece together why his face looked so recognizable.

"First things first. Coffee or tea?" he asked with a large smile.

"Tea...always tea," I said as I reached for the mug he offered me.

"Got it. I'll have to remember that for next time," he turned around and went into the kitchen.

I sat next to Saoirse who was laid out on the couch with a blanket over her head. "Who's the cute guy?" I asked. Oops, did I just say that aloud?

"I heard that," the mystery man yelled from the kitchen.

Saoirse said something that was mumbled under the blanket.

"I'm sorry Saoirse, I cannot understand anything you are saying."

She took the blanket off her face and in a monotone voice replied, "This is Mateo. He's annoying but good people. He's like my brother."

"Thanks, Saoirse really appreciate the hype," Mateo yelled from the kitchen. "You sang with me last night, remember?"

Oh gosh, I thought that was all a horrible dream. "Did I really...?"

"Did you really sing Brittany Spears in an Irish pub to a crowd of drunk people? Why yes, yes you did Leena and I've got to say it was pretty incredible," Mateo came in and set a plate of french toast covered in peanut butter and syrup with a side of mac'n'cheese.

"Hm,....thanks," I smiled and moved the french toast around with my fork.

"Oh, come on, give it a try. It'll cure that hangover of yours."

Anything to cure this throbbing in my head. I politely cut off a piece of french toast and chewed it slowly. The peanut butter was warm, gooey, and so delicious. It tasted so good. "I can't even remember the last time I had peanut butter," I said as I began to scarf down the french toast.

"I had an American roommate a couple of years ago and he always made me this exact plate of food every time I was hungover which, at that time, was quite a bit. I think I gained 20 kilos that year," he explained.

I stopped and put my fork down.

"What? What's wrong? Did you find a shell?" Mateo asked.

"No, nothing. I'm fine. This was delicious and very sweet of you. Thanks, I really appreciate it." What was I supposed to tell him? That I didn't want to gain weight, that I meticulously calculated my portion sizes, that I didn't have the freedom to just eat anymore or that I would probably do a million sit-ups after they left to burn off the piece of french toast I already ate?

"Ok, well there is more in the fridge," he said as he looked intently at me. No one had ever looked at me this way, not that I had noticed at least. It's like he actually liked me. Is that silly to say? Gosh, I feel like a child blushing from embarrassment.

"Ok, love birds," Saoirse got up and headed to the kitchen.

"Saoirse, you're ruining the moment," Mateo yelled as she walked by. "Anyway, Saoirse told me you are studying writing. That's cool!"

"Ya, it's something I've always wanted to do," I said as I snuggled into the corner of the couch.

"I'm actually kind of in your program," he said, "I'm studying poetry, so we might have some of the same classes. Maybe we can study together or something."

"Ya, maybe," I said, covering my face in a blanket.

"Is everything ok?" Mateo asked.

"I just realized what I look like," I got up and headed down the hallway, "Saoirse? I'm getting in the shower," I yelled from the living room. "You can stay as long as you like but I have to be at work by 2."

Mateo looked at the clock on his phone. "Well you better hurry, it's 1:30. And don't worry, you look beautiful."

"1:30!" I ran into the bathroom and wiggled my dress off.

Saoirse threw a pillow at Mateo, "What? she is! Just saying."

When I left, Mateo was in the kitchen cleaning while Saoirse was trying to convince him to let her style him. Those two were quite the pair and truly bickered like brother and sister even if they weren't technically related.

I arrived at work just in time to open the shop with Eloise. She took one look at me and smiled. "I think you have a story to tell," she stated as she watered the daisies in front of the store window.

"Eloise, you are not going to believe my night."

Chapter 9

To my future self,

I love my writing program! My advisor is this older man who looks like Indiana Jones. He's in his eighties and everyday wears a hat that I swear is straight out of the movies. He even has an old leather bag that he totes around. He's wonderful and has really been pushing me to be authentic in my writing. To show parts of me in every character and every setting so that every story I'm sharing parts of myself. It's really challenging, especially since I'm not quite sure who I really am. Is that normal? I would have thought I would have figured that out by now. I guess that's part of the process, being honest that is.

I still miss Trevor. I crave him in ways that can be debilitating. Like I'll be at the store and run across his favorite snack and I'll find myself surrounded in a memory. Transported back to an event that I didn't even feel like was important at the time. And everything will feel real. I hear sounds, smells, and feel pain; it's jolting. And it'll happen in an instant.

This last time I was at the grocery store, I saw this particular type of beef jerky that he always ate on game nights. As soon as I smelled it, my surroundings changed. All I could see was him sitting in front of the TV eating his jerky and drinking a Heineken. I could hear him screaming at the game. I could taste the beer as he forced a kiss on me when his team scored. I could feel his arms wrapped around my body. In that moment, I felt him. It's like he never left. Just a normal Sunday night. But in an instant I jolted awake at the sound of a toddler knocking over a can of beans. I began to panic. The air seemed to escape my lungs with every passing second and my body began to shake. The boy's mother asked if I was ok. I nodded my head yes as I quickly ran out of the store. I found an alley and knelt down putting my head on my knees. Water streamed from my eyes soaking my jeans with tear stains. It took me a good hour before I felt like I could move and when I finally made it home I just laid in bed feeling physically drained.

It's crazy because one day I'll feel completely normal like I never met him and those three years have just been erased and then other days I feel his presence. I can feel him on my body, in my mind, he's just there. He wasn't all bad. Sure he might have done some awful things to me but aren't we the most horrible to those we love the most? Isn't that some right of passage for being in a long-term committed relationship? You suffer the bad in hopes of finding something good?

He was cold, but he was sweet too. He often would bring me home carnations just because. I mean my favorite flowers are deep red roses, but it's the thought that counts. And, when we were in bed and he rubbed his hands down my body and whispered I love you in my ear, I felt wanted and seen. He knew exactly what to do to make me feel good, to make me feel like we were together, to make me feel like I was safe in his hands even if it was just for a moment.

He would grab my ass when we were laying down saying he had never been with a woman like me before and that he didn't know what he did to deserve me. And, I just wanted to make him happy, to make him feel good and loved the way he made me feel. Sure, that slowly faded but the thing with my relationship with Trevor, when it was good it was really, really mind-blowing-over-the-moon good. And when it was bad, it was the deepest heartbreaking-earth-shattering mind-crushing bad. There was no in between with him. He was hot or cold, but never lukewarm.

Everytime I lay alone in bed craving his cuddles, his body, his smell, I'm reminded of Sarah. Is this how she felt all the years when he was with me? Or was she with him the whole time? I once found lipstick in his suitcase. When I asked him about it he told me it was mine and that I was being ridiculous, but I never wore pink lipstick, I only wore red. I don't know what hurt more, the fact that he didn't know that, or the fact that he was most likely sleeping with another woman; or women. He was gone a lot and I just looked at it as a sacrifice I had to make to be with him. Another decision he got to make. Besides, I could do more, be more, to make him happy. If he needed another woman I was somehow not enough and I could be enough if I just tried a little harder. At least that's what I told myself over and over until it became the reality I believed. I can be enough if I just try a little harder. I pushed the thought of another woman away, knowing that one existed but believing it to be untrue. But when I saw her, when I experienced her beauty, it became real. She was real.

Simon tried to call a couple of times but I deleted the voicemails before listening to them. I didn't have the emotional bandwidth to reopen that wound. Maybe it never really healed. Maybe my exposed and raw heart from Trevor's death distracted me from the pain of Simon. Maybe our whole relationship did. Afterall, Simon was my first real love. I had been with him since I was a kid and we were only broken up for a short time before I met Trevor online.

It didn't matter though, I wasn't enough for him either. He didn't choose me. He chose himself and now he had chosen his wife, and there was nothing I could do about that and nothing I really wanted to do about it either. I know what it's like to lose a father. Even though I had a bad one, it was still hard. I still love him and I still miss him and it hasn't really gotten easier even though he left so many years ago. I wasn't enough for him either. I was not going to take Simon's little girl's father away from her and I'm not sure I even wanted him anymore or if he truly wanted me. You don't just leave someone you love, right? Even if they don't fit anymore. Or did I get that wrong all these years? I can't stop thinking about Trevor and his lasting legacy in my life. To be honest I didn't really want Simon, I wanted Trevor. I needed him. I wanted to feel him again, even if only for a moment. I couldn't think about any other man, only him. I want to want again, to feel again, but I just can't. My mind, my body, is so used to Trevor, so infatuated with him that I can't pull myself out of the grief that keeps me close to him.

I'm not sure why I'm writing all this down. I've had to do a lot of introspection in this program and things keep popping up. My therapist says it's good and that I've shown a lot of resilience so I guess I'm making progress. It just doesn't really feel like that yet. I'm not sure it ever will.

On another note, Saoirse has been an incredible roommate. We have a good rhythm and have roommate dinners once a week which is a big deal because her school load is crazy! She is designing her own fabric. I know, cool right? She teamed up with this girl who is in the science program and they are doing a joint thesis. We just started our program and they already secured funding for next semester to test out their formula. Saoirse is of course planning this big fashion show right down the middle of Eyre Square. That girl goes for what she wants, that's for sure.

I've made a good friend in Mateo. He is kind and sweet and everything I don't deserve in a friend. Even though my heart still belongs to Trevor, part of me wishes it didn't. But I am lucky he sticks around even though I try to push him away. He's patient with me, which is not something I'm used to and not something I'm sure I know how to handle. Pursuit without conditions, without expectation... it doesn't feel right. I told him I'm only looking for friendship and he seems ok with that and honestly I was shocked by his kindness and the support he's been giving me, considering I just met him not too long ago. The night I freaked out at the grocery store I called him. I don't know why. I just did. And he told me to take a deep breath and focus on the things I could see and hear and I just started to calm down. He showed up later that night with groceries. I couldn't get out of bed, but he let himself in and put them away. I found a note the next day that read, "Today may have been hard, but there are many tomorrows that will be better. I hope you enjoy the chocolate covered strawberries. I heard they were your favorite. See you in class tomorrow. - Mateo"

We actually have all the same classes. I didn't realize this but the writing program is very diverse, so I get to learn a bunch of different types of writing but emphasize a speciality, which for me is creative writing. Mateo's emphasis is poetry but we have all the same classes at this point. We are taking a poetry workshop together, but I'm not sure I like it. It's very challenging and I'm not sure I'll pass. I want to ask Mateo for help, but I'm embarrassed and don't want him to read more into the request. He's already done so much for me and while I feel like I've known him for a long time, it actually hasn't been that long. He brought me a chai soy tea latte (my go-to drink of choice) with a teddy bear for Valentine's Day. Very sweet, but I didn't want to lead him on. He gave me no reason to believe he wanted something from the gift or with anything he did for me, but don't men always expect something? Doesn't everything really come with the expectation of something else? I'm trying to be careful. I'm still really broken and I don't want my shards to cut too deep into Mateo or into the parts of me that are trying to heal. Besides he deserves better than me, better than what I can give him.

Chapter 10

To my future self,

I haven't heard from mom in awhile. Dad said she's alright but has the flu. Something feels off, but I'm not sure what it is. I've asked the family and everyone has said not to worry. I leave for home in just two months. I was going to stay through the summer, but something is telling me to go home. And if I have learned anything from my mother, it's that you follow your gut because your gut is just your soul telling you what it needs.

My job at the shop is going great! Eloise is so sweet and thoughtful. She invited me to the countryside next weekend to meet her sons and grandkids. I think it might be a fun adventure. I've never been to the countryside before. It's weird that I still haven't met her son. He goes to NU, but I haven't bumped into him yet. He picked something up from the shop one day, but I guess I was in the back room and just missed him. Eloise was very disappointed. I think she wants to set me up with him. That's the last thing I need right now.

My writing program is getting more challenging. In my poetry workshop I have to travel to a place picked at random with a partner and then write a poem about the experience or place. I, of course, partnered up with Mateo and we were given The Cliffs of Moher which I was really excited about because I'm pretty sure a scene from Harry Potter was filmed there, and who doesn't love that cult classic series. We leave tomorrow. Saoirse is coming too! First, we'll explore the cliffs then we'll catch a ferry to the Aran Islands. We're making a whole day out of it.

I have packed my rain jacket and snacks for the journey. but for some reason I'm a little nervous. I have unexplainable butterflies that make me want to throw-up. I guess I'm just really excited to explore. I haven't done much of that since I've been back.

To my future self,

Today was hard but I guess most good things are. At least that's what I'm telling myself. Saoirse, Mateo and I climbed into our red tour bus ready for the day's adventure. We sat right behind the bus driver because I get motion sick and I didn't want to vomit on the lovely bus full of travelers excited to see The Cliffs of Moher.

Our driver's name was Sean. The whole time he went on and on about how his daughter married a protestant and how it was so devastating to her Catholic family. But they ended up loving him and now they have grandchildren and he didn't know he could be so happy with a protestant in the family. It was all a little comical and jarring at the same time. I grew up in a house with a Catholic mother and a protestant stepfather and never really considered their difference in religion being a source of conflict. Maybe for them it wasn't. But Ireland, from my limited knowledge, has historic trauma relating to protestant and catholic disputes, but don't quote me on that because I have no idea what I'm talking about.

I found myself staring out the window. I had never seen such green grass before. It seemed like it went on forever. It was separated into squares and rectangles by long lines of stones stacked together making a natural looking kind of fence. It must have taken forever to make that! It was so beautiful.

I eventually fell asleep to the lulling motion of the bus. I woke up snuggled in Mateo's arm. He was out cold. I slowly moved his arm off mine hoping not to wake him. I didn't want him to get the wrong idea. Saoirse popped up and smiled deviously.

"What?" I said as I put my rain jacket back on.

"What's ah going on here?" she replied, pointing her twizzler at us.

"I just fell asleep, that's all."

"Mhkay. You keep telling yourself that. But you remember Leena, he's a good one. You don't have to worry about him."

"I never thought I did," I said as I stood up accidentally jolting Mateo awake.

"Are we here?" he asked as he stretched awake.

"Oh, ya, Leena and I were just…"

"Don't you dare Saoirse! I mean it," I said, shooting daggers at her with my eyes knowing she was about to say something to Mateo that would completely mortify me.

She smiled and put her hands up, "Ok, ok. Leena and I were just saying that we should get some photos of the place Harry Potter was filmed at."

"Ya, we should," he replied. "Great idea!" he was probably used to Saoirse's behavior enough to know when to drop something, and I'm sure my red face probably gave me away anyhow.

The cliffs were breathtaking. The salty breeze kissed my face and pushed my body back with each gust. The sound of splashing waves was surprisingly loud considering how high we were. I left Saoirse and Mateo and started to ascend the stairs to the visitors' center. I wanted to get some souvenirs to bring home to my family.

The building was like nothing I'd ever seen before. It was built into the hill with only the stairs and exposed windows showing. I went up to the counter where a jolly man asked if he could do anything for me. I gave him the small trinkets I had found in the shop. Before checking out he asked me if I wanted to look up my family crest. I'm guessing he saw the American passport when I reached in my bag to get my wallet and since most Americans are into this sort of thing it wasn't too presumptuous to try to upsell me the product.

I thought for a second. My father was Irish. His family migrated not too long ago. He was only 2 or 3 generations removed. There could very well be a family that lived in the area that I was related to. For all I know, this man could be my uncle twice removed.

My father was a hard man. He was kind too, but only when he wanted something or his appearance was threatened. Even at a young age something in me didn't let me fully trust him. I can't explain it. And when he got angry his eyes turned black, and his face shook. That's when I knew his rage was taking over. I would try to hide but he would always find me. As he yelled names at me he would sling my small body around. I numbed myself trying to escape the pain, the terror. When he finally left my mom and I, I can say that I honestly wasn't surprised. And even though I love him and miss him because he is my father, I'm done being angry at him. He left, and yes it affected..affects...me but it also brought me my real dad, Tony. The only dad I ever really knew and his big loud family that I love. While he is technically my stepdad, there wasn't a day I didn't feel like his biological child. Not a day he didn't make me feel safe. Not a day he didn't make me feel loved. And even though he always showed up, I can't let go of all the horrible things my biological dad said and did to me. He broke me. I would never say any of this to my mom or Tony. I wouldn't want them to feel like they failed. No, this was my fault. Why couldn't I shake him? Why couldn't I just let it go? Pretend nothing ever happened? Pretend he was the perfect father like everyone around me seemed to want me to do. The community remembers him as this pillar, this steadfast man who always sacrificed for others. My mom doesn't mention him at all. But to me, his words slice through me everyday. His beatings, fresh in my mind every morning as I travel back to that little girl hiding from him in the closet, covering myself with clothes so he wouldn't find me. I can't escape him. I can't move on and I'm not sure I can pretend everything is ok anymore. I'm tired of the lie.

I turned my attention to the salesman. "Sure," I said before I even realized what I was saying. "Last name ó Conchobhair and first name James."

The man smiled as he entered the name, "It's unusual to have a proper last name and not a shortened version these days. Makes things easier for me." The man was quiet as he punched letters into his keyboard. "Ah, here it is. Would you like it framed or rolled?"

Wow, had he just found my family crest that quickly? How could something I've run from for so long find me so easily. "Rolled, please," I replied.

"Would you like to see it first?"

I thought for a moment. "No, that's ok. I'm fine. My friends are waiting."

The man smiled as he rolled the very official looking document and placed it inside a round cardboard holder. I paid the man, thanked him for his help and descended down the stairs.

What had I just done and why had I done it? Everyday I fought to be over my father and what he did to me. I mean he left so long ago, twenty-two years to be exact. For all I know, he could be dead or living down the road from me. God, I hope not. I'm not ready to see him. I'm not sure I'll ever be. This document wouldn't tell me anything about him. It's just a family crest, but for some reason I wanted to know so much more. Who were his parents? His school bully? What had made him the way he was and why was I never enough? Buying this crest felt somewhat like a beginning, but I'm not sure what kind; a path to healing, or a descent into another round of depression and anxiety? I'm not sure I'm ready for either.

I met up with Saoirse and Mateo and the rest of our group and we headed off to catch our ferry to the Aran Islands. The bus driver explained to us on the way that the population on The Aran Islands was dwindling because the young people don't want to settle there. They go off to university or want to live in the city where there are more things to do. He explained that the people are very close to each other and that most of them are Fishermen, so there have been a lot of men lost to the sea. He also recommended the ice-cream at the only bakery on the island. He said it was the best dessert he had ever had, especially with a slice of pie.

We got to the ferry just in time, but the captain wouldn't let Saoirse on. He said red heads were bad luck and they were expecting a storm.

"What an ass," Saoirse said, "I'll show him back luck!" she screamed so he could hear it. The captain retreated into the ship. He was genuinely afraid of her. "It's ok guys. I'm going to take a taxi back. I need to work with my partner on the fabric formula anyway. We have to send our supply list to the dean by next week. You guys have fun though."

I gave her a hug, "I baked you cookies before I left. Chocolate chip, your favorite."

"You, Leena, are a saint!" She grabbed my hand and walked forward with me. "Don't do anything I wouldn't do," she said as she moved her eyebrows up and down.

"Saoirse!" I yelled, pushing her playfully.

"Oh, and Mateo. You better be a perfect gentleman to our Leena! Or not, show her a good time," she yelled as she got into her taxi.

Mateo blushed as he walked over to me. "Sorry about that. That's just Saoirse. Are you ready to get on the ferry?"

I nodded my head yes and walked up the slim stairs of the boat.

Surprisingly, I didn't get motion sick on the ferry. I was shocked but we actually talked the whole time about writing and art. It was nice to have a friend that got me. I don't think I've ever really had that before, not this way. When I first met him I knew there was something special about him. I thought I was just getting caught up in the music at the pub, but now I'm not so sure. He's really different, in a good way, I think. When we arrived at the island with our tour group we were left on our own to explore. I was excited for the hike up to the cliffs. The entrance looked straight out of an old storybook.

"Do you want to hike to the cliff?" Mateo asked. He could see me eyeing it.

"Sure," we began to ascend the old stone path that wrapped around the hills leading to the top. It was more challenging than I expected. Not too hard, honestly I just think I'm out of shape. As I climbed up the path my head began to pound and I started to sway, losing my footing. I hadn't eaten much all day and my body could feel it.

After walking for what seemed forever we finally reached the top of the cliffs. It was breathtaking. "Wow, this is beautiful," I said under my breath.

"Ya, it is," Mateo responded. "You know I've never been here before. Saoirse and I always talked about it, but never made it. It's always been on our list of tourist attractions to visit."

"Oh, I'm sorry. She should be here," I suddenly felt like I had somehow taken something away from her. "We could have waited so you could do it together. I didn't mean to be an imposition."

Mateo looked at me confused, "She did me a favor. I'm glad you're here with me Leena. I like spending time with you."

I looked away trying to hide my hot cheeks. I walked ahead of him silently so I could catch my breath from the hike up the trail. Further up the cliffs I found an abandoned rock out of sight from the other tourists. I climbed up the stone and gently sat down, my muscles relieved to get a break. Mateo sat next to me. "Mateo?" I asked.

"Ya, Leena," he looked at me as if waiting to hear an answer to an unasked question.

"Do you have any snacks? I left my carrot sticks on the bus and I feel like I'm going to pass out."

He smiled, "Yes, I always have snacks. I've been around Saoirse long enough to know to bring snacks anytime we travel together. Or just anytime at all. That girl loves her snacks, and she can be the most hangry person I've ever met," he pulled his bag off his back and onto his lap. "Would you like trail mix, chocolate chip cookies, or twizzlers?"

"Trail mix, please," I replied eagerly. I put a big handful in my mouth. Raisins, peanuts and sunflower seeds never tasted so good.

Mateo handed me his water bottle and I gulped down the remaining water like I had never had liquid in my body before. I let out a deep breath of satisfaction.

"Better?" he asked.

I replied with a smile. "Sorry, I didn't mean to finish your water."

"Oh, that's fine," he said as he reattached his bottle to his bag. He looked down at his hands that were interlocked, thumbs fiddling, "Leena, is it ok if I ask you something?"

"Depends on what you ask," I replied, not moving my eyes from the crashing waves.

"It's about us," I could feel him staring at me.

"I'm not ready for that question yet," I closed my eyes.

"Do you mind if I just hold you here while we look at the sunset?" he asked.

I looked at him and in that moment everything else melted away. Out of all the women who wanted him, who went to every show, that knew so much more about him, he wanted me. Why? This man was kind, thoughtful, and deeply cared for me in ways that were terrifyingly honest. Ways I didn't deserve. I had never experienced this type of thoughtfulness, this type of respect. At this moment Trevor, Simon, my dad, they all just disappeared from their spots as air traffic control in my mind. I looked at him and for the first real time, I saw him. His heart was painted on his face and that was the moment I knew I was in trouble.

Chapter 11

To my future self,

I got an A on my poetry assignment. I know I'm shocked just as much as you are. Mateo keeps asking me if he can read my poem but it's so personal. I keep changing the subject hoping he'll give up. He has insisted I read his, but I know that if I do I'll feel obligated to let him read mine, so I've avoided the topic and he has been a gentleman about it. For the most part. Maybe one day I'll let him read it.

Anyway, I leave for home in just two weeks. Part of me is so excited to see my family, especially my mom who I feel like I never get to talk to anymore, and the other part of me is really sad because I've made my own sort of family here in Galway. As a last hurrah, Eloise has invited me to her son's house in the country. I'm finally going to meet that grandson of hers who I still haven't met. Saoirse can't make it to the party, but she is sending me with a bottle of wine. I guess she actually knows Eloise and her family. Small world huh? I'm going to miss her and our adventures. She is staying in our flat for the remainder of the year so the plan is just to rejoin her in the fall. I'm only taking a month break so I'll be back a whole month early to help Eloise in the shop.

Saoirse lent me a beautiful blue sundress that had a slight white floral pattern. She paired it with white strappy heels, a sun hat and of course my classic red lipstick. I'm actually really excited to meet Eloise's family. I feel like she's my grandmother and because of that they are somehow family I haven't met yet.

So here's to tomorrow! And to going home in just a couple of weeks!

To my future self,

Eloise drove us to the country in her little bright yellow bug. I thought we were going to die at least 7 times, but we arrived fashionably late. Her family was lovely. Her sons were kind and funny and you could tell they all really loved each other. And I did finally meet her grandson.

"Leena, I want you to meet my grandson, Conor. He's also a student at NU," Eloise handed me a glass of beer as I chatted with her grandson.

"Hi, nice to meet you. I think my grandmother likes you more than me," he said jokingly.

"Well, she visits me more," Eloise said as she handed him a fresh beer.

"Grandma, that's not fair. She works in your shop."

"You could work in my shop."

"I've got school."

"Leena has school," she snapped back.

"I'm sure Eloise loves you even more than she loves me. And I assure you, I am so fond of your grandmother. She has been so kind to me," I said as we both laughed at their exchange. Eloise threw her hands up and walked over to newly arriving guests.

"I'm really glad you started working at her shop. The place looks great and I know she appreciates the help," Conor said.

I nodded my head and smiled. "So, you go to NU? I'm surprised I haven't seen you in passing. What are you studying?"

"Oh, I tend to stick to the science building. I'm studying biology. You're a writer, right?"

"Hhm, I don't know. Hopefully one day. I am studying writing though."

"Well, you write, correct?"

I nodded yes.

"Then that makes you a writer. You don't need others telling you what you are and aren't, right?" He was witty, I'll give him that.

"You sound just like my roommate Saoirse."

"Saoirse is your roommate?"

"You know her?" I was surprised.

"If you are talking about the Saoirse with bright red hair and an equally shocking personality then yes, she has broken my heart a few times. We grew up together. She is well, Saoirse. And I love her for it."

"Me too. She said she knew Eloise and her family. So, I guess this makes sense," I replied. I guess I shouldn't have been too surprised. The Galway countryside isn't too big. I don't think it is at least.

"Yep, we all grew up together in this small village," he took a drink of his beer, "So you're the Leena that Mateo talks constantly about then."

I could feel my cheeks getting red.

"Ah, so you do like him then," he said, noticing the color in my face change.

I didn't know what to say. "We…ah…he's become a really close friend. I see him just about everyday."

"You have stolen my friend away, Leena Estrada," he stated with a smile.

"I have done no such thing," I sipped on my beer and rolled my eyes. "But I do really like getting to know him. We've had some fun adventures."

"Well, he certainly is enjoying getting to know you," Conor said as he raised his eyebrows and took a gulp of his beer.

"What's that supposed to mean?"

"It means, put the man out of his misery. He obviously is in love with you and by the look on your face you seem pretty smitten as well. In fact, you know what, hold on just a second," Conor pulled out his phone. "I just happened to know that Mateo is home visiting his mom this weekend because he is a decent man who loves his family, another great quality about him," Conor dialed a number and I presume Mateo answered on the other end. "Mateo, hi, it's your dear pal Conor. I happen to have Leena here at my house. Hmm. Yes. Why? Because she's friends with my grandma. I know. Crazy. Anyway, I was just telling Leena how smitten you were and...calm down...I know...I know....well, I think you should just come on over and smooth this thing out, right? Ok, see you soon. Oh, bring her there? Good work, Mateo. I think she'll love it."

"Hey, 'she' is right here!" I reminded him.

"Right, right," he said, shooing me away. "Ok, Mateo I'll give you twenty minutes and then I'll lead her to the spot. See ya soon champ," Conor hung up the phone. "See it's all taken care of."

"You and Saoirse are more alike than you know," I said as I finished my beer.

"We really are," he said as he stared out into space. "You'll be fine," he looked down at me. "Now go mingle and I'll come find you in a bit," he gently touched my elbow as he walked beyond me.

Him and Soairse were either going to end up passionate lovers or mortal enemies. Maybe both I guess.

I passed a table of food and met more of the family while I anxiously looked at the clock. I was so nervous to see Mateo. Why had Conor gone and stuck his nose where it didn't belong? Things were good between Mateo and I. Manageable, predictable, and I liked that. But I had a feeling that was all about to change, and part of me was really excited about that, but most of me was terrified and confused.

After what seemed to be a lifetime, Conor finally found me. He took my beer and placed it on the table, "Ok, he's ready. Let's go," he grabbed my hand as we headed for the backdoor of the little house. "Grandma!" he shouted.

She looked over at him, "I'm taking Leena. Mateo will take her home later."

She smiled, "Have fun dear. I'll see you in the shop tomorrow."

I ran out of the door with Conor, "Thanks, Eloise!"

We exited the house and walked down a dirt path. After walking out of the gate we slowed our pace, which I was grateful for. I hate running, a lot. We walked through an old wooden gate and reached another direct path. It was filled with views of rolling hills covered in bright yellow flowers. "Wow, it's so beautiful. It must have been something to grow up here."

"Ya, I had a really great childhood. Soairse, Mateo and I were inseparable. We went on many adventures."

I smiled.

We continued to walk for about five more minutes before he stopped me. "Leena, I know you are a good person. Eloise doesn't just trust anyone in her shop. Up until you it was family only. So, I'm trusting you with this bit of information. Can I trust you?"

I shook my head. Had I somehow become an FBI agent or something?

"Good, I thought so. This path leads to a very special place. No one except Mateo, Saoirse and I have been there. It was our secret hiding place as kids. It's a big deal that he's bringing you here, so if your feelings aren't mutual please be kind to him. Can I trust you to do that?"

I nodded my head and kissed him on the cheek, "You're a good friend Conor."

He stepped forward and moved some ivy that showed a whole in the stone fence. "Follow the path, he'll be waiting for you in the fort."

"The fort?"

"Bye Leena. I hope I'll be seeing more of you0," Conor turned around and headed back to the house.

I followed the path for what seemed like forever, but I didn't mind. I felt like I was in a storybook. The forest was mesmerizing. I could hear birds calling to each other and I could see butterflies moving from plant to plant. Green moss covered the forest thicket and then out of nowhere an abandoned short castle appeared. It's stone walls were mostly missing and covered by the hill. There was only one torrent left and Mateo was standing at the entrance with red roses.

He smiled at me as I walked towards him.

"Hi," I said, slightly shaking.

"These are for you," he handed me a bouquet of flowers. Red roses...how did he know those were my favorite? He took my hand and guided me to a picnic blanket he had laid in the middle of the dilapidated castle. There was a picnic basket with wine and cheese waiting for us. We walked over to the blanket and he poured me a glass of water.

"Mateo, this is all...too much. I mean no one has ever..." I couldn't finish the sentence. No one has ever done anything like this for me before. Nothing this kind, this incredibly detailed and sweet, all on a moment's notice. He really knew me and he really cared about me. I was starting to understand how much. "How did you do all of this in such a short time?"

"Well, the picnic stuff is my mom's. I had brought food home from the market and made due with what I had, and there is this kind lady and her daughter that live at the end of my street. They have a ton of rose bushes and let me cut a few for you."

"Wow, you really thought of everything," I said, doing everything in my power to hold it together.

"Leena, I need to tell you something. You know when we went to The Aran Islands...can we finish the conversation now?"

My body went numb and I began to cry uncontrollably. What was happening to me?

Mateo held me for a long minute and then gently pulled away so he could see my face.

"What's wrong Leena? Did I say or do something to upset you? If so, I am so sorry. We can leave if you want. Go back to the party or I can take you home. Whatever you need."

I cut him off, "No, that's the point. You've only ever been so kind to me and so wonderful. Nothing can be this good, this right. You're going to change. They always do. And if somehow you don't then maybe....maybe I just don't deserve you, ok?!" Still wrapped in his arms I turned my face away from him.

He wiped my tears and gently brushed my hair behind my ears. "Leena, I'm not Trevor, or Simon, or your father. I'm me and I am so crazy about you," he took my face in his hands, "I fell in love with you that night on stage when I saw this quite cute girl, who I knew Saoirse drug to my show, dance and have fun, even though she didn't know a soul at the pub. The girl who always takes care of Saoirse even though she is a rollercoaster of a person. The girl who has such a kind and generous heart and is so talented and beautiful."

Beautiful. He thinks I'm beautiful. I thought back to that night Saoirse said something that still stuck with me, I get to decide what happens next.

"Leena what I'm trying to say is...I"

"I love you, Mateo," I said, cutting him off. "I'm sorry. I just love you and I couldn't wait another moment to tell you," I spit out with a shaken voice staring at the ground.

He pulled me in close and kissed me so deeply I thought my heart was going to burst. My face grew hot and I felt like I was spinning. His lips felt warm, his tongue inviting. I had never been kissed like this before and I knew from this day forward I would mark my days by this day, by this kiss, by this moment. For the first time, this first kiss felt like a beginning and an end.

Chapter 12

Dear Mateo,

You deserve better. I love you enough to let you go.

Leena

Dr. Trite

Poem Final

I miss you.

Sometimes I search for you in a crowd because,

I miss you.

If only I had been less proud because,

I miss you.

Sometimes I wish he never broke me because,

I miss you.

If I had a cavalry because,

I miss you.

Sometimes I think of what could of been because,

I miss you.

The things I've missed no telling when because,

I miss you.

Dear childhood, I'm sorry you're over now,

And I know I'm somewhat guilty somehow,

because forever,

for always,

I'll miss you.

To my future self,

It's been a few days since I've been home. So much has happened. I don't even know where to begin. When I got home my mom was laying in her room. Her hair had thinned and she looked so small and fragile. My dad told me she was doing chemo and radiation for kidney cancer. They removed the cancerous kidney and were doing treatments to ensure all the cancer was out of her body.

I was so angry and so hurt and so sad for my mom. She just laid there weak. Like every breath might be her last. All I could do was hold her and scratch her head the way she scratched mine when I was a child sick with chickenpox.

"Leena, welcome home. I'll have to make you tamales to take back to your friends," she said with exhaustion in her breath.

I hugged her tight, "No, mom. It's my turn. It's my turn to take care of you."

She buried her head in my arms, "I'm glad you're home sweetie, but you can't stay forever. You have too much life to live."

"You are my life mom. I'm here."

She might have had her last chemo and radiation treatment, but I knew looking at her that she would never be the same. I never really thought about what happens to cancer patients after their treatment. I always assumed life somehow just went back to normal for them. But now I realized there isn't really a happy ever after, just a happy I survived but my life has changed forever. I knew more than ever she needed me and I owed her my everything. She had made mistakes, she didn't always put me first in the ways I needed her too or keep me safe in the ways motherhood demanded, but she did her best and she was the best, the best she could be and that was enough. I had forgiven her for him and because of that she had become not just my mother, but my closest friend. I couldn't even comprehend life without her, without us, not after I lived without her for so long. I had just gotten her back, losing her was not an option. She would be ok, even if I had to will it to be so, the universe owed me that, right? I guess it doesn't really owe anyone anything, but I was hoping just this once I would get what I wanted, what I needed. Her.

Chapter 13

To my future self,

Mom is doing better. The doctor says her numbers are good and that she is on the path of recovery. She won't hit remission until her 5 year mark and until then they will consistently check her numbers. She gained enough strength to walk and eat but she's not her usual self. Her glow has faded and I'm afraid I may lose my mother forever. That doesn't keep her from being the force of nature God created her to be.

"Leena, when does your flight leave for Ireland?" she asked. I was curled up in a blanket beside her.

"Oh, don't worry about that mom," I replied as I started to paint her nails, still warm in the big blue blanket my little brother bought her for her birthday.

"Leena, you know I love you right?" she said, looking down at her nails. "You know I want my baby here with me every moment, right?" I wasn't sure what she was getting at. "You can't use me as an excuse to stop living your life. I'm fine. I'm not going anywhere."

I thought for a long second as I tried to work up the courage to say what I needed to say next. "And, how can I trust you?" it came out more harshly than I meant. I could tell the words hurt her. "I'm sorry, I didn't mean it to sound that way. I just mean how can I trust that you'll tell me when you're not ok?"

My mom looked at me apologetically.

"You know, we are a team. When father left it was just you and me until you married dad. We were always a team and I know I hurt you with Trevor but I just....I have to know you are ok. I can't live without you again. We tell each other things. You're my best friend, mom. I won't lose you again," I said.

She squeezed my hands, "Leena, you never lost me. Not really. And even in death I will be haunting you," we laughed through tears, "I love you. I am so sorry I hurt you. I just didn't want to take away from your healing journey. You just seemed so happy. Happier than I have ever seen you. And I wanted to make that last as long as I could," she gave me a hug and a kiss on the cheek. "I think it's time."

"Time for what?" I questioned.

"Sweetie, grab me my bible off the dresser, please," she said as she pointed to the old family bible that had been passed down generation after generation.

I grabbed her bible and gently handed it to her.

"Now, hold it here," she said as she moved my hand holding the bible in front of her.

"Ah-hem," she uttered, clearing her throat dramatically. "I, Maria Rosa Garcia Estrada, solemnly swear to tell Leena, the first real love of my life, when I am struggling."

I smiled.

"As long as she agrees to not use me as an excuse to not live her life."

I rolled my eyes, "Ok, ok you've made your point. What do you want to know?"

"What's his name?"

I let out a deep exhale, "It doesn't matter. I messed everything up."

"If he's right, he'll still be there. Tell me about him."

"Well, he's kind and sweet and thoughtful, and everything I didn't know I needed and even more than anything I ever imagined."

My mom smiled, "he seems very special."

"Ya, but that's the problem. He's too perfect. He can't be real. And even if he was, I'm not sure...never mind," I bit my lip fearing I had said too much.

"What sweetie...? You can tell me," she said, rubbing my back.

"I'm not sure I deserve him. I'm not sure I can be loved by someone like that."

"What do you mean? You are wonderful."

I could feel tears slowly streaming down my face.

"I'm not, mom. I'm not enough. And, I don't know how to be enough. I wasn't enough for Simon, he left me. I wasn't enough for Trevor, he cheated on me more than I probably even suspected, and..." my mom wiped my tears from my face with the back of her finger, "And he left...he just left."

"Who left? Trevor?"

"No, dad! My real father. One day he was here and the next he just left. And if he can't love me...if he chooses not to love me and he is my parent, the only man biologically designed to love me, then how can I ever expect someone else to choose me?"

"Oh, Leena," my mother hugged me tight, "Your father had a problem."

"Ya, me," I said through choked tears.

"No baby, not you. You are a blessing, a beautiful blessing. I think it's time I told you the whole story."

I looked at her in confusion.

"I didn't think you needed to hear it because you just clicked so well with Tony I thought maybe he could be enough for you. That I could shield you from the pain."

"I love Tony. He's been the best dad I could have asked for but..."

"But you need to know. It's time. You're ready. And it seems like your soul is guiding you to answers," my mom sat up straight in bed with a serious look on her face. "Ok, I can be ready to tell you," she pointed to her first dresser drawer. "In that dresser is a white shoe box, can you bring it to me?"

I handed her the shoe box and snuggled next to her in bed. She opened it slowly and a musty smell filled the room. She clearly hadn't opened the box in years. She pulled out a photo of Abuela and grandpa and handed it to me.

"This is Abuela and grandpa. As you know, Abuela was from Texas. She was Mexican and my father didn't really know his heritage but thought he might be Spanish and German from stories his mother told him as a child. Grandpa died when I was just fourteen. And in my grief I rebelled. One night at a party I met this boy. Leena, I'm ashamed to say this, but I didn't even know his name. He was kind to me in a time when I just wanted to feel anything but pain," she handed me another photo of her and a man sitting around a bonfire drinking beer. "This is the only photo I have of him. Your aunt drunkenly took it with a camera your grandfather had bought for her. This, Leena, is your father."

I froze in shock. My body couldn't decide if it wanted to explode in rage or stop breathing. I could feel my head getting hotter.

My mother must have sensed my reaction, "I slept with him out in the woods. Honestly, I don't know anything about him. We were both drunk and I don't remember all the details from that night. It was my first time. I don't know what town he was from or why he was at the party. I don't even know if he was my age, Leena. And, when I found out I was pregnant I was terrified, and so was abuela. She thought that the community would treat me differently if they found out I was pregnant, so I agreed to an arranged marriage. Oisin agreed to marry me with the condition that we have more children and I live on his farm. He was much older than me, Leena. The only way we could legally get married was to have my mom sign a paper giving us permission to marry. It was a different time. No one even questioned it."

I was in shock, this couldn't be. She handed me a photo of her pregnant with Oisin on the farm we lived on so many years ago.

"Abuela thought Oisin was a good man. He went to church. Always tithed. He was quiet but always showed up to volunteer when the church needed something. So when she asked him to marry me and he said yes, Abuela thought everything was solved."

"Was she ashamed?" I regretted the words as soon as they left my mouth. "I'm sorry mom, I didn't mean it like that. You had nothing to be ashamed about."

"No, no. It's ok Leena. You deserve to have all your questions answered. Maybe, but I don't think so. I think she was mainly worried about how the community would treat me and how she would provide for me and you. Your grandfather had just passed away and she was working double shifts at the grocery store to provide for me and your uncles and aunts. I think she thought she was doing me a kindness and you a kindness by finding us a good person who would take care of us."

She pulled out another photo. This one was of Oisin and another woman. "Who's that?" I asked.

"That's the woman Oisin loved. Her name was Emily. See, it's printed on the back."

I turned the photo over and it read, "Emily, my love. I can't wait for our forever."

"Wow, he was really in love. What happened to her?"

"I don't know. But it seems like I wasn't much of a substitution for her. Oisin loved you and in his own way loved me. At least the best he could.

But he had his own issues. When he started hitting me I took it. I thought I deserved it. I thought this was the life I asked for and the only way to protect and provide for you. But when he started to hit you. I knew something had to change. One day while he was out I packed up your things and walked six miles to Abuela's house. I showed her our bruises and she said I never had to go back. When Oisin showed up later that night he was apologetic. Abuela wanted none of his excuses."

"Did she feel guilty for marrying you to him?" I asked.

"She never said so, but I could feel she did. Wouldn't you? Sometimes as a parent you are just trying to do the best you can do and hope your decisions are right and provide the best for your child. Even though her decisions hurt me, I forgave her. Not because I had to, but because I loved her and she changed. She saw that what she did was wrong and she never did anything like that to me or your aunts or uncles ever again."

"What happened to Oisin?" I asked.

"This might take you by surprise, Leena. Are you sure you want to know?" she said hesitantly.

I shook my head slowly. She pulled out another photo of two young girls on the beach together. They looked familiar but I couldn't quite recognize who they were.

"This is Abuela and her best friend Eloise."

My head began to pound as I put the pieces together. The woman looked familiar because she was my Eloise. My substitute abuela. "I....I don't know what to say," I hopped off the bed looking at her with hurt written all over my face.

"Please, Leena. Let me tell the rest of the story."

I could feel my body getting hotter. That meant Eloise knew this whole time. She knew my mom was sick and she didn't tell me! Rage paced through my body. "How could you? I thought. I thought. I thought my soul had brought her to me. How ridiculous is that!? I feel so....so stupid." I ran out of her room and through the house.

"Leena! Leena! Please, come back. There's so much more! Please, wait!" she cried out as I slammed her bedroom door behind her.

I couldn't believe what I just heard. Not only was my childhood much different than I thought, my dearest friends in Ireland had been lying to me the whole time. Were they all in on it? Saoirse? Mateo? I mean they all grew up in the same village. That couldn't be a coincidence. Was I just their pity project?

I walked out of the house and down the cement sidewalk. I grabbed my phone and dialed Mateo's number.

It rang only once.

"Leena! Leena, is that you? Are you ok? I wanted to call, but wasn't sure if that was ok."

"Was it a lie?" I asked, my voice shaking.

"A lie...was what a lie?" he questioned.

"Us, was it a lie? Were you in on it?"

"Leena, I'm not sure what you are talking about."

"You know. Us. Was I just a project? Someone for you to fix? You know, 'Poor Leena, she needs a bit of excitement.' Was Soirse in on it too?"

"Leena, I have no idea what you're talking about. Are you ok?" his voice sounded concerned.

"Come off it. Eloise knew and she's Conor's grandma, and your bestfriends with Conor and Saoirse, so were you all in on it? Were you just trying to make me fall in love with you? Is that it? Just a sick game?"

"I think you're overestimating my relationship with Conor's grandma."

And then it hit me, he had no idea what I was talking about. This man. This beautiful soul filled with nothing but kindness and generosity towards others would never be capable of purposely hurting another person.

"Never mind. I'm sorry Mateo," I said embarrassed as I quickly hung up the phone.

"Leena!" Tony called from the front door. "Leena, where are you?" he said as he walked down the front yard looking frantically for me. He spotted me and sighed with relief. "Leena, what are you doing?"

I silently shook my head at him. "Did you know too?"

"Know what?

"That Oisin isn't my real dad?" I asked accusingly.

"Of course. I'm your dad."

I squinted my face knowing that I had just hurt him and for the first time I saw Tony for what he was. The man that chose me everyday. The man that chose my mom everyday. The man that read me stories to sleep. The man who attended every choir recital, every graduation. He was part of every big moment in my life. And suddenly, nothing else mattered. My whole life I thought there was something wrong with me because Oisin left, but I never realized that Tony chose me everyday not because he had to, but because he loved me and he loved my mother. It was better than biological conditioning, it was his choice. He would be the man that I would dance with at my wedding. He would be the man my children would call Abuelo. He is the type of man I should feel like I deserve. I ran to him and gave him a big hug, "Thank you, dad."

"For what, mijah?"

"Everything."

Chapter 14

To my future self,

It has been quite the week. I found out that my mom got knocked up, was pretty much forced to be a child bride and that Oisin wasn't my real dad. Oh, and that Eloise, my Eloise, was best friends with my abuela. Not only that, after my little episode outside, my mom refused to tell me anymore about the story until this morning after a couple of guests arrived.

Saoirse marched in my room shouting my name, "Leena? Leena, where are you?"

I woke up out of bed rubbing my eyes, surely I was dreaming. Saoirse couldn't be standing over me in bed? Right? "Saoirse is that you?"

"Of course! Who else has my voice and stunning sense of style?"

I stood up and gave her a hug. "What are you doing here?" I asked.

"Well, hello to you too. Your mom called Eloise and she thought you may need a friend. And I have beef with you. You are breaking my dear Mateo's heart and that simply just won't do."

I gave her another hug and filled her in on what had happened with my mom just a few days before. "Wow, so Oisin wasn't your father? And your mom was in an arranged marriage? You, Leena, are much more interesting than you give yourself credit for. Well, this simply won't do." She grabbed my hand and barged in the kitchen where my mom was having coffee with Eloise.

I gave Eloise a hug. Even though I was mad at her, I still missed her.

She grabbed my face and said, "It's good to see you dear."

"Wait, El, you have a lot to explain. And, so do you," Saoirse said as she eyed my mom up and down.

"I like her," my mom said to Eloise. "She's a spitfire."

"No, I'm a whole goddamn forest fire." Saoirse said with a smile. "Ok, this is when you both start talking."

I grabbed Saoirse a cup of coffee, and we sat around the kitchen table waiting for the rest of the story to begin.

"Your abuela Maria was a strong woman. She was kind and gracious, but she always told things how they were. I admired her for that. She also was very adventurous and beautiful. It wasn't easy for her growing up in Indiana as a Mexican woman. People often used racial slurs around her, and she never really felt accepted by the community. In that time, there weren't too many families like hers in the town we lived in and I knew she felt isolated. But there is more to the story than both of you know," Eloise looked at my mother. "What you don't know is that Maria was raped when she was fourteen by her school teacher. She didn't tell anyone except me. She was scared and wasn't sure anyone would believe her, and she had her reasons to anticipate that reaction."

My mom looked hurt. Eloise sensing my mom's pain grabbed her hand. "Your mom never told anyone. Not even her parents. She only told me because of what happened next," Eloise took a sip of her coffee and looked around at the circle of women. "It was a different time then. The power imbalance between men and women was even greater then, and as a Mexican woman living in a small midwestern town, your mom feared that if anyone found out it would endanger her and the child she was carrying. Maria and her family lived on my father's land. Her father was the Farm Manager for my family's land and our families became close."

"I remember," my mother said as if remembering something long forgotten. "They let us stay on the farm rent free when my father passed away."

"Yes, and my family would have done more if they could. They got your mom a job at the grocery store they sold inventory to, but that was a tough season for the farm and my father regretted not being able to do more. He loved your father and always considered your mom a second daughter. I remember as a kid he would sneak us popsicles and candy. He was a good man. Anyhow, Maria wore really baggy clothes to hide her stomach, and she never really got too big. So, no one even suspected she was pregnant. One night your mom got really intense cramps and went into labor. She knocked on my window scared. We went to this big abandoned barn on the land and she gave birth to a baby boy. He was so small. He fit in just one of my hands. He was too small. So fragile. He came out motionless and blue."

We were all silent in shock.

"I had been birthing cows since I was a child so I knew the gist of things. I helped your mom deliver the placenta and cleaned her up. I'll never forget the way that child looked or the silence between us. She held her baby boy until she drifted asleep from exhaustion. I buried him underneath the willow tree while your mom finally slept. It was her favorite place, so I knew she could visit him often there without suspicion. I woke her up just before sunrise and snuck her back into her house. After she told me about the father, we agreed never to talk about it."

I never knew the pain abuela was carrying with her all these years. I never knew she lost a child or that she was raped.

Eliose turned to my mom, "She always assumed you were raped at the bonfire, and you being the same age that she was raped brought up a lot of pain for her. She felt like she failed you. When you became pregnant she didn't want you to experience the loss of losing your child. She thought if you weren't married you might give Leena up for adoption. She also feared how the community would treat you. She wasn't sure you would be safe physically or emotionally so she did what she thought was best for both of you. When she told me what Oisin did to you and Leena she felt like she failed you all over again. We had to make a plan to get him as far away from you both as possible. My husband Cain got him a nice job at a farm a couple of towns away from our village in Galway. He had some distant cousins there too. Maria told him he had to go. He agreed. Out of guilt or shame, I'm not sure, but he sold his farm and moved to Ireland."

I felt dizzy by the haunting thought that the man who had caused me so much pain, so much fear, was probably only a few towns away from me in Ireland this whole time.

"My father helped Maria with your divorce papers and that was that. Oisin never came back. And..." Eloise hesitated for a moment. "Oisin died a couple of years ago. His wife and daughter found him one morning on the couch. He had stayed up watching television and had a heart attack. He's gone."

A weight fell heavy on my chest as I tried to choke down crying until I just erupted. Saoirse held me.

"Leena, are you ok?" Saoirse asked.

I shook my head no. My mom and Eloise hugged me until all three women were cradling me.

"It's ok, Leena," my mother said as she kissed my head.

"I just feel..." I couldn't say the words. "I just feel...." I mustered up all the courage I had left in my body, "I feel the same way I felt when Trevor died..."

"And what is that?" my mother asked gently as if she already knew what I was going to say, but knew the importance of me saying it aloud.

"Relief."

For the first time I said the word, and it released something deep inside of me. Something that wasn't exactly tangible, but needed to be let out from its cage.

"Me too," my mother said as she held me.

"It's ok," Saoirse assured us. "That doesn't make you terrible people. It just makes you human." She looked at me deeply once again, "You'll be alright, they can't hurt you anymore."

After we were done crying together we decided we needed to visit my abuela's son. We bought daisy's, my abuela's favorite flower, and laid some at his grave. My mom said a few words about how she wished she could have met him, and that one day they would meet in heaven and she would read him books and go on treasure hunts like she did as a kid with her brothers and sisters on Eloise's family farm. Then we went to my abuela's grave and left the remaining flowers. Eloise left her a handwritten letter and my mother told her she missed her and thanked her for doing the best she could. That she was a great mother and that she had never failed her.

That night we painted our nails and put on face masks like preteens at their first slumber party, except we slept and slept hard. Emotional rollercoasters really do take a lot out of you. For the first time in my life I felt light. Like there were possibilities I couldn't see before today.

Chapter 15

To my future self,

I woke up feeling refreshed and empowered. And then it hit me. There were things I needed to do. So, I grabbed my purse and the truck keys and walked swiftly out the door. As I drove down the old roads in Summer, Indiana I couldn't help but see this small town differently. Not only for the secrets it held but for the generational impact it had on my family. It had grown over the years from a one stoplight town to a booming area filled with new housing developments, restaurants and shops. It grew and changed in the same ways I had grown and changed but somehow it seemed different, I was seeing it for the humanity it held instead of the place I lived. In all its ugliness, it was also beautiful.

And then I arrived. As I pulled into the drive-way I couldn't help but feel anxious. I remembered what Saoirse said, they can't hurt you anymore. I took a deep breath and knocked on the door. After a few noises inside the door swung open.

"Hello, Michelle. It's nice to see you," I said.

"Leena? Is that you?" she questioned in a rude tone.

"I don't mean to take up too much of your time. I just wanted to check on you, see how you were doing and get an address from one of Trevor's friends."

She looked at me suspiciously. "Why would you care how I'm doing?"

"Well, you were a big part of my life for the last couple of years and I do care about you."

Michelle rolled her eyes, "You can't have any of his stuff. I'm sorry. He wouldn't have wanted you to have any of it anyway."

I clenched my fist tight trying to tame my anger. "What is your problem, Michelle?"

She looked at me in shock. I had never spoken like this to her before.

"I was so kind and so good to Trevor even though he was pretty terrible to me. I did everything you ever asked me to. I always did exactly what he told me to and still...still you are so horrible to me. What did I ever do to you?"

She let out a loud sigh as if annoyed. "Trevor was a good man and he deserved to be with someone he loved, not you."

"Wow, that is incredibly cruel. Your son was many things, but one thing he was not was a man that deserved any woman."

"Well, I never..." she muttered. I quickly interrupted her.

"Yes, you never. You never showed kindness. You never showed empathy. You never showed anything other than rudeness and selfishness, and you know what? I pray everyday that you have a happy life filled with love and kindness and people who fill you in ways you have never been filled before because that kind of meanness, that kind of hurt is only born out of pain and I wish so much more for you than that. I forgive you, but I'm also done with you. Goodbye, Michelle," I turned to walk away and she ran out the door and grabbed my arm.

"Wait. Wait! I'm..." she paused.

I waited while she stood there staring at me in silence. I turned and walked towards my truck.

"Wait!" she screamed. "You don't know, do you?"

"Don't know what?" I questioned.

"Do you have time for a cup of tea?"

I looked at her curiously. "Is this a trick?"

"Wait here, I'll be back," she said as she began to walk back into her house.

A few minutes later she came back with two mugs of tea. As I sat on her cement stairs drinking my mint tea my mind started to wonder. She had never offered me anything. I was almost afraid to drink it. After what seemed like forever she finally spoke, "You know living in a small town has its benefits. I've always loved being a Hoosier. The smell of autumn leaves in the fall, bonfires in the backyard, the excitement the whole community feels when the Pacers beat the Bulls. I've always loved living in Indiana. But everywhere in Indiana feels like a hometown. Everyone knows everyone, from Fort Wayne to Lafayette, you become something and it's hard to become something else. You know?"

I shook my head in acknowledgement. She wasn't wrong. The state had an unspoken camaraderie among its residents, for better and for worse.

"I didn't grow up in Summers. I grew up in the northern town Monticello. You might know it for Indiana Beach," she started to sing the small theme park's slogan and began to laugh.

It was strange. This was the first time I think I ever saw her smile. "It's a beautiful quaint town. It kind of reminds me of the town from Gilmore Girls. That show is probably way too old for you to know."

"Actually, I love that show. My mom and I have seen every episode at least four times. She had me when she was young so we bonded over it. You know?"

She smiled at me, "The town has parades just about every month and there is just an unshakable feeling of community there, although the town has its fair share of secrets. But those aren't for me to share. What I'm trying to say is, I loved that town and I loved the summers. Summer days on the lake, root beer and fried mushrooms at B&K, late night movies at the drive-in; it was great. I would go to Indiana Beach with my girlfriends just about every weekend even if it was just to get some Dippin' Dots and watch the boat show. One day I met this boy. He was sweet and generous and very handsome. He kissed me on the swinging pirate ship ride and we were inseparable all summer. When I met him, I changed. It's like I had met my person and I knew, I just knew I would never be the same. He swept me off my feet. We got married and had a son. He was the love of my life."

"Wow, that's beautiful. I didn't know you and Hank met as kids."

"We didn't."

I looked at her in confusion.

"Hank and I met when Trevor was seven. We met at the supermarket shopping for vegetables. Tevor's real father is Jerry. He died in an accident at work. He's the only man I've ever really loved other than Trevor. Jerry and I...well...his wife died around the same time Jerry died and we just kind of...exist together. I don't expect you to understand."

"Trevor never told me. I'm sorry," I said as I reached for her hand.

She pulled away, "I don't need your pity."

"That's not...ok," I replied.

"Trevor looks exactly like Jerry and every time I saw him it's like part of my heart rejoiced while the other part shattered all over again. I loved every moment with my son but he unintentionally brought me deep pain. Except when he was with Sarah, she reminds me of myself in some sense and you and I, we're just very different. And sometimes, I just....I don't know....don't know how to act around the women he loves, especially when they're different from me."

"You knew about Sarah?"

"Of course, he told me everything."

"Why, then? Why didn't he just leave me and stay with her," I said quietly.

"I think he loved you both the best way he knew how. As a momma you want the best for your child. But I know he was a difficult man, and I know he didn't always treat you right and for that I'm sorry. No sense drumming up the past, it's time to move on. So go, and don't come back around here checking up on me. I'll be just fine. I always have been and I always will be."

I shook my head and headed to the car.

"Leena, wait!" she screamed.

I turned around.

"What address did you need?" she asked.

"Oh...well, I was hoping you would give me Sarah's address. I have something I think Trevor might want her to have."

"I don't know if that's a good idea, child. Might be best to let it go."

"I know he loved her and I know that he was with her while he was with me. It's not about that."

Michelle shook her head, "Hold on," she ran inside and came back with an old receipt that had an address scribbled on the back.

"Here, now please don't be bothering me again. And Leena, let Trevor pass through you. Don't let him get stuck. Don't do what I did. You can do better, for us both."

"Yes, ma'am."

As I got back into my red family truck I gripped the black steering wheel and took a deep breath. I slowly pulled the receipt out of my sweater pocket. Indianapolis. That wasn't too far of a drive. I told myself. I can do this. I can do this. I can do this. I told myself over and over, trying to convince myself I could be strong enough to talk to her.

The drive seemed endless. In reality it was about half an hour. As I walked up to her apartment door my heart pounded. Part of me wished she wouldn't be home. But then she answered.

"Leena? Is that you? I'm so glad you are here. Please, come in," she welcomed me into her gorgeous apartment that was decorated in soft pink tones and vases of carnations. Photos of her and Trevor hung all over the apartment. It was weird seeing him as a college student and then as a grown man next to Sarah. I started to see a part of him he never showed me, and that shot a deep pain into my stomach. I took a seat on the white velvet couch and drank some water from a bottle that she handed me from a mini fridge in the living room.

There was silence for a moment as we sat on her big white couch. I could tell both of us were nervous about what to say. "I uh..wanted..."

Sarah cut me off, "Before you say anything I just want to apologize. It was completely inappropriate for me to ask for Trevor's necklace. It was insensitive and I shouldn't have said anything. I'm so, so, so sorry!"

I nodded my head, "Thanks. It's really ok. You were grieving just as much as I was. Afterall, you were his girlfriend too."

Her eyes widened, "How did you know? How long have you..."

"It's ok. I'm not mad. I knew when I saw you. That pink lipstick you're wearing, I found a tube of it in his suitcase a year or so ago. I only wear red so...when I saw that pink lipstick at the funeral and thought back to his 'business trips' it just clicked."

"Leena, I'm so sorry."

"Stop. It's really ok. Trevor was a dick. We both deserved better."

"He loved me, Leena. He was a good man," Sarah said, upset at my comment.

"Was he though?" her face dropped. I didn't want to cause her any more pain than she was already feeling. "It doesn't matter anymore. I'm sure he loved you. You can be a dick and still love someone. Anyway, I'm not here to argue with you about Trevor."

"Why are you here?" She questioned.

"I think he would have wanted you to have this. And I honestly just don't need it anymore. Here." I took off Trevor's old gold necklace and placed it in her hands. Wrapping my hands around hers. "He really loved you. You know that he wore this everyday. I'm not sure why he chose to be with me publicly. Honestly, I was never enough for him. But he wouldn't have worn this everyday if it didn't mean something to him. If you didn't mean something to him. While I hate him for hurting me, and I'm angry that you would choose to be with him knowing he was in a relationship with me, I don't blame you. You weren't in a relationship with me. He was. You're not responsible for my feelings. I am. What he did to me isn't your fault and I refuse to become a bitter woman who hates other people because of being hurt. I'm better than that. So, here. I don't want it anymore," I slowly slid off the pristine couch, stood up, and walked over to the door.

"Leena," Sarah said, catching my attention.

"Yes," I replied.

"I really am sorry. And he did really love you. If he didn't, he wouldn't have chosen to stay with us both."

"Maybe, but I deserve a better kind of love than that. And so do you," I closed the door and once again walked to my red family truck. Boy, had we done a lot together today. As I drove down the cornfield roads I felt released. Trevor didn't own my body anymore. He didn't own my heart anymore. He didn't own my mind anymore, and he didn't own my grief, and that was freeing.

For the first time in years, I finally felt like I could breathe.

Chapter 16

To my future self,

Today I had to make a choice, go back to Ireland with Saoirse and Eloise, or stay home with my mom and family.

"Mom," I said, laying on her lap as she scratched my head.

"Yes, Leena."

"I've made a decision and I need you to support me. Before I tell you, will you promise you won't fight me on my choice?"

She took a deep breath, "Whatever you need."

"I've decided to take a semester off and be here with you and the rest of the family. Now, before you say anything, remember you are a woman of your word and you already agreed not to fight me on the decision. And, it's too late to change my mind. I already talked with my advisor and he supports my decision. He will leave a funded spot for me next year if I choose to come back."

My mom smiled, "So, it's done then."

I shook my head yes.

My mom grabbed my head and held me close, "I've missed you Leena. More than you'll ever know."

"I just can't lose anymore time with you. I barely saw you the first year Trevor and I were dating and then I didn't see you at all for the 2 years we lived together. And then I went off to Ireland and almost lost you forever."

My mom hugged me tighter, "I'm right here sweetie. I'm right here. I won't fight you now, but if your happiness is for one second jeopardized by you staying home we're fighting. You understand?"

"Yes, ma'am."

As I gave hugs to Eloise and Saoirse my heart ached. They had become my best friends and I honestly didn't know the next time I would see them.

"Are you sure the shop is going to be fine?" I asked Eloise as she put on her cardigan.

"Oh yes, the shop will be fine. I'll be fine. Everything will be fine. Remember, I've got grandsons who will want their inheritance."

I laughed, "Thank you so much for coming and for everything you've done for me and my mom. You are family. I will write to you every week and I want the inside scoop on the romance between this one," I point to Saoirse, "and your sweet grandson."

Eloise smiled, "That sounds lovely."

"No romance exists...yet at least. He's the type of man you settle down with, and I'm the kind of woman who eats men like that," Saoirse replied.

"There will be no eating of grandsons, Saoirse," Eloise said as she leaned over to me and gave me a big hug goodbye, "I'll keep you filled in. Don't you worry," she whispered. "Ok, girls I'll be in the car."

Saoirse hugged me and leaned her head on mine. "I'm going to miss you Leena. You have become my closest girlfriend. Usually girls don't get on with me but we just...fit."

"I'll miss you too, Saoirse," I squeezed her tight.

"Well, I better be seeing you next year at Uni. Wasn't going to mention this to you but I got approved for another full year of funding!" we both jumped up and down screaming.

"So, you have to be my roommate next year. I won't take no for an answer."

"You have a deal. If I come back that is."

Saoirse looked at me confused.

"It's just that my mom, she's sick, and honestly I just miss my family."

"Poor Mateo will be heartbroken," Saoirse replied.

"I know. He's so wonderful. Truly. He's sweet, and kind. And we have so much in common. He reminds me a lot of my stepdad…which is a good thing. He's everything I could never allow myself to dream of but…"

"But nothing. You two are perfect for each other," she said abruptly.

"Maybe, but he deserves a whole person and I'm just not that. Not yet at least. I need time."

"Ok. But remember we're all beautifully broken in our own ways. Human connection isn't about fitting two perfect people together. It's about using our broken pieces to make a path that we can both walk together."

"Saoirse, that was beautiful."

"That's what Mateo always tells me when I talk about Conor. He's a good man and he loves you."

"I know, but I have to love myself before I can let someone else in and I'm just not there."

"Ok. I support you whatever you decide. But remember, it's your decision."

I gave her a big hug, "Thank you, Saoirse. I wouldn't be where I am today without you. I really wouldn't."

"Me either friend," she wiped a tear and pointed her finger at me, "Now, you don't go singing at pubs without me, ok?!"

I smiled and shook my head in agreement.

"I'll see you soon on video chat. I demand at least one weekly conversation," she said.

"I think two is a better number," I replied.

"Sounds lovely! I'll call you when we land and I'll make sure Eloise gets home."

And just like that, Saoirse was out the door and on her way back to Ireland.

Chapter 17

To my future self,

My aunts came over today to make tamales. My brother's birthday is next week and we needed to prepare so there was enough food. It's one of my favorite family traditions. All the women in my family get together and make my abuela's tamale recipe. Sure, we each have our own variation, but when we make hers it's like she's in the room with us and in our own way we honor her memory and everything she taught us by making her recipe and teaching it to the new generation of women. Today was very exciting because my two little cousins were helping for the first time. They were so excited when we put them on husk duty. They cleaned each husk as they watched my mom make the masa dough.

"So, Leena, your mom tells me you have a boyfriend back in Ireland," my aunt asked.

"Mom!" I yelled.

"What, you know I tell my sisters everything."

The women laughed.

"It's nothing to be ashamed of Leena," my other aunt shouted over the sound of boiling water.

"Well, he's not my boyfriend, but yes, I did meet someone," I replied.

"Oooohhhooooo!" my little cousins said as they started to pat masa dough on the clean dry corn husks.

"And why is he not your boyfriend?" my aunt asked as she added more pepper water to her batch of the masa mixture.

"Well, I'm just not ready, and he's all the way in Ireland and I'm here so I just don't see it working out right now," I replied.

"Did I ever tell you about Quan?" she asked.

I shook my head no.

"I met him right after high school. He was so handsome and such a good kisser. I mean that man could make my whole body tingle with just one kiss."

"Eww, mom! That's so gross," my little cousin yelled.

"Sweetie, you have to learn about these things one day, and I'm your mom but I'm also a woman. I have needs," my aunt retorted.

"Gross, I don't want to hear about your needs," my little cousin said as she continued washing a new batch of corn husks. "Can you please not tell me this story mom?"

My aunt rolled her eyes, "Anyway, Quan and I dated, for what, about 2 years or so?"

My mom nodded in agreement, "He was a dick."

"Mom!" I said in shock. I never heard her say anything like that before.

"What? I call it how I see it. He was a dick,"

"Well, he definitely had a big dick," My aunt replied as she and her sisters laughed.

"What has gotten into you guys today? There are children present." I said as I shewed my cousins away with ice popsicles.

"Leena, he was...earth shattering in all the right places," my aunt did a little dance.

Tamale time was always like this. My mom and her sisters telling crazy stories as they drank wine and danced to whatever was playing on the radio.

"One day I caught that son-of-a-bitch with that tramp…what was her name again?" my aunt looked at her sisters.

"Haley, I think. Or was it Kirsten. Maybe it was both," my mom laughed as she poured herself another glass of wine.

"Anyway, your mom and I bought three packs of pads and put ketchup all over them and then stuck them to his green corvette," they laughed together.

"That man was too scared to touch them. He drove his car five miles down the road and through downtown to make it to the car wash where he paid some guys to take them off," they burst with laughter, all of them with tears streaming down their faces.

"We got him so good," my aunt said hyperventilating with laughter, "I have to sit down, I'm going to pee myself," she said, not able to stop laughing, "I asked him…" she tried to catch her breath, "I asked him how his cycle went the next day and he hung up the phone," she burst out with more laughter.

"He learned his lesson…or maybe he didn't…but we felt better," my aunt said as she finally caught her breath. "Anyway, I'm telling you this story to say that there are jerks out in the world. And they suck. But not every guy is a jerk. If you want to be single, be single. If you want to be unattached so you can find yourself, be unattached. But if you are choosing to be single because you are afraid of love, then you're missing out on life. Don't let the Quans of the world prevent you from finding happiness. You deserve it whether you think you do or not."

My aunts surrounded me with hugs.

"Thanks, I missed you guys," I said as we stood hugging for a couple of minutes before my mom started to snore, "Mom, wake up. How much wine have you had?"

"What? I only had a few glasses," she replied.

"Ok, I think we should pick up our tamale making tomorrow," I said, breaking the hug circle. "I'll clean up. You guys go drink a glass of water or something."

My mom and my aunts walked into my mom's room laughing as they reminisced.

Chapter 18

To my future self,

I talked to Mateo today. My heart began racing as the phone started to ring.

"Leena, I was hoping you would call. Is everything ok? Saoirse wouldn't tell me anything and I wanted to respect your boundaries so I didn't call, but I've been really worried. Are you ok?" he asked.

"Hi, Mateo. It's really good to hear your voice. I've missed you. I'm sorry, I didn't mean to worry you. I'm ok."

"Good, I'm glad you're alright. Do you know when you're coming back? I can pick you up from the airport if that's ok."

"That's really sweet of you. I need to tell you something though," I said nervously. "Do you have time to talk for a bit?"

"Of course," he replied.

"First, tell me about your summer. How are things going?"

"Uhmm, ok, well Dr. Clatch gave me a really great opportunity to be his TA this summer. I've been teaching an undergraduate summer writing workshop. It's been really great and I've really connected with my students this semester. I'm really excited about it. But enough about me, How are you? How's your family?"

"That's really great Mateo! I know how much something like that means to you. Congratulations, really! That's incredible. I'm doing better, much better actually and my mom is doing good. Her numbers are up and the doctor's think all the cancer is gone."

"That's great!" he replied.

"But, I need to talk to you about something and it's really hard for me. I've been working up the courage for days."

"Ok, I'm listening," he responded.

"My mother is doing much better, but she still needs me and honestly I need her. Almost losing her scared the shit out of me. She's my best friend Mateo, and I just can't leave her. Not now."

"So you're not coming back?" he asked.

"No."

"Not ever? Or not this semester?"

"I don't know."

"Oh, I see. And you're sure about this? That this is what you want."

"Yes. I'm sorry Mateo and I'm sorry I acted crazy on the phone a while back ago."

"You weren't being crazy. You were going through a lot. I get it," he said with a deep sadness in his voice.

"Thank you for understanding. This is something I have to do even though all I want is..." I paused silently for a minute.

"All you want is what?" he asked.

"I can't. Not yet."

"All you want is me?"

"I can't, Mateo."

"Why? Just say it Leena. It's ok. I'm not going to hurt you. I feel it too and I know you do. I see the way you look at me. I feel it in your lips. I feel it just being with you, Leena. The prickles on my skin when you touch me. The feeling like my heart is going to explode everytime I hear your name and I know it's scary. I'm scared too. I've never felt this way before."

"Mateo, I can't," I replied. I didn't want him to say something that would put me on a plane, and take me thousands of miles away from my family.

"What if I move there? That way you can be with your family and I can finish my studies online or find a good grad school close."

"No," I said without thinking.

"Why not, Leena? Don't you want me?" he asked.

"Of course I do," Oh no, was I making him feel like Trevor made me feel? Like Simon made me feel? Like Oisin made me feel? "Mateo I am so sorry. I never wanted to make you feel like I didn't want you," It was just hitting me that my behavior toward him may have been confusing to him. I was a mess and he was getting hurt from it.

"Then what? That night in the woods, did it mean as much to you as it meant to me?"

"Of course it did. It was so special and I'll always remember it and you."

"But it's not enough. You don't even want to try?"

"I can't," I replied.

"Why not, Leena? I can wait if you're not ready."

"I can't do that to you."

"That's my choice, and I choose you if you'll choose me back," he said with desperation in his voice.

"I love you too much to ask you to put your life on hold for me. I won't do it. I won't ask that of you."

"Don't you get it, Leena? You don't have to ask because I love you."

"It's not enough."

"It could be," he pleaded.

"No, I'm sorry Mateo. I have to go," I hung up before he could say any more. I was barely holding it together and the more he talked the more I wanted him. The more I wanted to give it a try. And I couldn't. All my life I've let men control me. I know he's different. I know he's kind and that he loves me in a way that no other man has, but it's not enough. I have to be enough for myself. I need to be stronger. I need to find myself before I can give myself to someone else again. I don't want to be consumed again with something toxic, because losing Trevor almost killed me and if I lost Mateo like that…I don't know what I would do. It's easier this way. You can't lose something you don't have.

Chapter 19

To my future self,

Today was an interesting day. I'm trying not to think of Mateo, but I have to be honest, it's very hard. I don't think I've ever felt this way about someone before and I fear that I've lost any potential future, even friendship, with him. I haven't reached out because I don't want things to be harder for either of us then they need to be. He stopped calling after a few weeks of me not answering the phone. And Saoirse has been so busy with her research project that I haven't been able to get a hold of her.

Anyway, my therapist suggested I do things to bring me joy. So, I've begun to read again. I used to love to read but Simon hated it so I kind of grew out of the habit and lost my passion for it. I don't think Trevor even knew I liked to read.

I got a job at my local library. I really enjoy reading to the little kids that come in for storytime. I found this book the other day when I was checking that the books were in the right order. It's called, Love and Gelato. It was in the wrong place. The cover caught my eye and I turned over the book to read the synopsis. I was hooked. I read the book all night and it really inspired me. It's like the book was written for me. The main character is also called Leena and her mom died suddenly of cancer. The book is about her grieving the death of her mom as she discovers more about herself and her father in Italy, guided by her mother's journal. She was on a journey to discover who her father was to help her figure out who she is. I haven't finished it yet but it really moved me. It got me thinking, maybe I should find my biological father. I mean, just to know who he is.

"Mom, I need to talk to you about something," I said as I jumped in her bed kicking my stepdad out of the room.

"Ok. What is it? You're pregnant?" she smiled. That was our inside joke she would say to bring some comedy to heavy topics I was nervous to talk about.

"I want to meet my father," I blurted out.

"Oh. I was not expecting that," she said as she took her reading glasses off.

"It's just that, I don't know, I feel like I'm supposed to meet him."

"Ah, ok."

"OK? just like that?" I was shocked.

"Sure."

"It's that easy."

"Well, I've kind of been trying to figure out how to tell you something?" she said.

"You're pregnant?" We both laughed. "Seriously though, what?" I asked.

"Well, when you found out about your biological dad I thought you might want to meet him, so I started looking for him."

"Oh," I didn't understand why she thought I would be mad about that.

"I kind of, sort of, took your saliva from you while you were sleeping and did one of those genetic test things."

My chest started to burn, "You did what!?"

"I know it sounds crazy, but I didn't want you to feel pressured, but I also wanted you to have the information if you ever asked for it."

"Mom!" I screamed. "You crossed way too many boundaries. You can't just do that!"

"I know. I know. I'm sorry! I wasn't thinking straight. I'm sorry," she said while squinting her face.

I took a deep breath. "Promise me you will never do anything like that again. You have to have my consent for things like that, mom. I'm not a kid anymore."

"You're right. I'm sorry. It won't happen again."

"Well?" I questioned.

"Oh, right. I found him. He was in the database. And guess what?"

"What?" I asked, beginning to get annoyed by all the secrets.

"He lives in Grand Rapids but is originally from Canada. Turns out the night we met he was visiting a potential host family for a study abroad which fell through. He's actually a professor at GVSU."

"What?! My old school? How is that possible," I asked rhetorically.

"I've been in contact with him for about a week and he would really like to meet you."

I sat quietly. I didn't know what to say. I didn't know how to feel.

"Leena. Leena, are you ok?" my mom asked worriedly.

"I'm just...surprised that's all. And I can't believe you talked to him without talking to me first."

"I'm sorry, he popped up and I reached out through the app and we exchanged numbers."

"Does dad know?"

"Of course. They have talked too. Everything has been great. He seems like a very nice man, Leena," she said.

"This is too weird."

"What? Your dad loves you and he agrees if meeting your biological father helps you in any way he is all for it."

At that moment my dad walked in the door with milk and cookies, my favorite snack, "My girls are so beautiful," he said as he laid the tray of food in front of us.

"That was perfect timing," My mom said as she gave him a kiss. "I just told Leena about the test."

"Did you know she was going to do that?" I looked at him demanding an answer.

"No, and I was upset too. She crossed a line," he responded.

"Thank you! So I'm not crazy."

"No, you're not. That was completely inappropriate and your mom knows that now and promises she won't do anything like that again," he said.

"Honestly, I kind of wanted to find him too just to see how he was doing. To see if you had any brothers or sisters you know," my mother said as she grabbed a cookie off the tray.

"What?! I have brothers and sisters," I yelled.

"No, no sweetie, you don't have any brothers or sisters. Your biological father doesn't have any other kids."

"That he knows of," I said sarcastically as I took a gulp of milk.

My mom continued, "He's never been married, but is engaged to a professor at the school and he's an academic like you. Teaching philosophy I think?"

"No, I think he teaches Art History," my dad replied.

"You guys, this is crazy. Dad, you're ok with this?" I asked.

"Of course. If it's what's best for you, then I'm ok with it. I don't need blood to know I'm your dad Leena."

I gave him a big hug.

"So, you want to meet him?" my mom asked me.

"Oh, I think that would be a good idea," my stepfather said, "Hey, I have to go to Grand Rapids tomorrow to pick-up a part for my car. I would be happy to drive you. We can make a date out of it. I'll even buy you chinese food at that place downtown that you like."

"Really, you would come with me? Just like that?" I asked.

"Of course, I love you. It's settled, we'll leave in the morning. I'll call James and work out the details. He'll be so excited to see you."

"James? His name is James?" I asked.

My mom smiled, "Yes, James Wheatly," that was the first time I heard my real father's name and in that moment my body wanted to shake and be still in a chaos of mixed emotion.

Chapter 20

To my future self,

My dad and I were unusually quiet as we made the four hour drive to Grand Rapids. I wondered who my biological father was. Had I seen him in the hallway when I was an undergraduate student? The name didn't seem familiar, but it was a big school. Maybe he worked at the downtown campus. Most of my classes were in Allendale so I could have missed him if that were true. What was his favorite color? Where did he go to school? When did he move from Canada to the states, was it a permanent move? How did he feel about my mom? I had so many questions I wanted to ask him.

"Are you ok Leena?" my dad asked kindly as we drove down midwestern roads in the red family truck.

"Ya, I'm just…I don't know," I replied.

"Nervous?" he asked.

"Ya, I guess I am."

"That seems like the most normal response to this kind of situation."

"I just have a lot of questions for him, that's all."

"Well, you could make this a regular thing. He doesn't live that far away."

"I'm not sure I want that. I already have a dad," I smiled at him.

"I appreciate that sweetie, but it's ok if you want a relationship with him too. It won't hurt me. You've got enough love for the both of us. I'll be ok. I promise."

"Ok," I replied. "Thanks dad."

We arrived just before 1 PM. As my dad parked in guest parking my hands began to shake. My father put his hands on top of mine, "It'll be ok. I'll be right here," he said.

"Ok."

"Are you ready?" he asked.

I shook my head yes.

We got out of the car and headed toward the library.

"I thought you might feel the most comfortable at the library. It was always your spot when you went to school here and so, I don't know, I thought it would make things easier."

I gave my dad a kiss on the cheek and a big hug, "Thanks, dad."

As we got closer to the entrance of the library my heart felt like it was dying. I could feel my whole body start to shake. I choked down the vomit that was starting to travel up my throat as we walked up the stairs to the big library doors. And then I saw him, a tall man with jet black hair and a light complexion wearing a suit and tie. He looked at me with familiarity as he rushed toward me.

"Leena is that you?" he asked.

I shook my head yes.

"May I hug you?"

I gave him a somewhat awkward hug. His embrace felt strange. It was new but familiar.

"And you must be Tony?" he shook my dad's hand, "It's so great to finally meet you both. Wow, you look exactly like your mother."

"You remember her?" I asked in surprise.

"Of course. We were both pretty drunk that night, but I remember her. She was the most beautiful girl I had ever seen. That's not something you forget easily. I've reserved a room in the library for us. Would you like to chat for a bit? I have all day. I cleared my classes so we could have as much time as you want. My students were excited for the day off."

"Ok, that sounds nice," I replied.

My dad and I followed James as he led us to the room he reserved.

"I love this library. It's probably the biggest library from any university I've worked at. I'll give you a tour after if you like. There's this cool hallway underground that leads you to the student center area. Pretty cool!" he said as he walked through the library.

"Oh, I actually went here. I'm a Laker. That sounds super corny. Sorry! I got my BA in Literature here," I said slightly embarrassed.

"That's crazy! Your parents didn't mention that. You know my fiance works in the literature department. Dr. Shelby Green. Did you have her in any of your classes?" he asked.

"What?! You're kidding right? She was my advisor! This is too creepy."

"Small world! I moved here two years ago to be close to her. We were long distance for about 5 years and I couldn't take it anymore. I teach in the Art History department now and get to see her everyday, obviously. Sorry, I'm a bit nervous," he said as he opened the door to the private study room he reserved.

"So, you're the Canadian man she always talked about, eh?" I said jokingly.

"I guess so."

"Wow, I thought you looked familiar. I've seen that picture of you two on her desk a million times," I said as we all took a seat at the table in the room.

"Well, before you leave we'll have to stop by her office and surprise her. She'll be shocked and honestly I would love to see the look on her face when she finds out you're my daughter. I mean she knows I'm meeting you today, but she doesn't know it's you, obviously."

"I like her. She was always really kind to me and her teaching style is so relatable."

"Ya, I think I'll keep her around," he said with a wink. "So I have a million questions for you and I'm sure you have a ton for me too. Do you want to go first or should I?" he asked.

"How about we take turns; a question for a question?"

"I like it!" he exclaimed.

"Hey sweetie are you going to be ok here with James?" my dad asked me, "Would you mind if I go and pick up that part real quick?" He stood up and shook hands with James.

"Sure, dad," I said as I stood up and gave him a big hug. But as I went to give him a kiss on the cheek I noticed his face was a little wet. "Just a sec James. I just want to talk with my dad alone for a sec. I'll be right back," We walked out of the room and into the hallway where James couldn't see us, "Dad, are you ok?"

"Yes, sweetie. I'm fine. I'll just be a couple of hours. Besides you and your dad need some time to get to know each other," he said.

"You are my dad. He is James."

"For now. And that's ok," he said.

"Dad, are you sure you are ok with this? We can go. Today can just be our day."

"Yes, sweetie. I will be fine. You go and have a wonderful day with James and I'll pick you up at four to get chinese. Sounds good?"

I wrapped my arms around him, "Thanks, dad."

As I watched my dad leave he seemed a little heavier. Like something had been taken away from him. But no one could ever take Tony from me. He was the one man who has loved me unconditionally from the moment he met me. Well the one man besides Mateo. I sat with James and talked about literature, and he was so excited I was in graduate school. He said he would pay for my Ph.D if I couldn't find funding and that I could apply for dual citizenship and get grant money through the Canadian government if I wanted to. He was so kind and so generous and meeting him was a reflection of all the parts of me I didn't share with my mom. He got me in a different kind of way. We were so similar and so different it was odd. I had his nose and height and passion for academics. I wondered what else we might share.

Dr. Green was so excited when she saw me and even more excited that I wasn't there just to catch up, but to be introduced as James' daughter. She would be my stepmother I guess....if that's what I want. And, it felt nice to already have such a good connection with her. It also made me feel better about James. Dr. Green is a really good person, a really strong person. She never settles for anything but excellence so I'm sure James meets that qualification too.

My dad, my real dad Tony, and I had a great daddy daughter night eating chinese and reminiscing about things we did together when I was just a small girl. I was filled with so much joy that I thought I would burst. I felt filled, whole. I felt ready. Like this was the final piece I needed, not to be me again, but to a different kind of me. It wasn't meeting James that did it, it was seeing how great Tony was through the whole process. He put me first. He did what was best for me even though it caused him pain. He fought for me. He's been fighting for me. He never stopped. He was a good man and if he thinks I'm worth that fight, maybe I am. It inspires me to fight for myself, for my happiness, and then all of the sudden my heart stopped.

Text: 8:05pm

Saoirse: Mateo has a girlfriend. Just thought you should know. Might be best if you don't talk to him anymore. I miss you lots. Let's chat soon. Love you!

Chapter 21

To my future self,

Saoirse words pierced through me deeply, slicing through every part of my healed heart and shredding it into pieces again. I had such a good day. I finally felt ready to let him in and he'd already moved on.

I thought he loved me. But how can you move on from someone you love so fast? He must have confused love with lust and now I feel so ridiculous. How could I be mad? I ignored him for so long. I wasn't ready. Maybe he stopped loving me because he needed to love himself and let go of the one person who was causing him pain. I let him go for this reason, because I didn't want to hurt him. Because I didn't want to be hurt and it didn't matter after all, because here I am hurt again. And part of me is happy for him because I love him so deeply that his happiness makes me happy and then another part of me is shattered because his happiness is with another woman which kills me.

I was ready to pack my bags and head back to Ireland, but now....I can't fathom seeing him with someone else. I guess it's better this way. There are grad schools here closer to home. Maybe I can finish up at GVSU. Get to know James better. At least it will be a distraction.

To my future self,

I've never been so confused. I feel like there are so many paths I could take and I'm afraid of choosing the wrong one again. I don't want to choose a path that is going to cause me pain or miss an opportunity that can't be replaced.

On one hand I've loved spending time with my mom and family. Being around them has been filling in an expected way. For years I had to tell myself that not seeing them was ok. That the trade off for love was worth it, and now I feel like an idiot because I had love all along. These people, these beautiful people, loved me, the real me, unconditionally and I was too wrapped up in my lack of self confidence that I couldn't see it or really feel it.

The love of the Trevors of the world was nothing compared to the love of my mom or my step dad or my brothers, aunts, uncles, or any of my big loud family. And I wasted 2, almost 3 years without them. How could I do that? I'm equally really pissed off at myself and really angry at Trevor for cutting them out of my life. I'll never make that mistake again. I won't allow myself to.

And now, I'm not sure if I'm staying at home because I feel this overwhelming guilt for not seeing them, or because I'm running away from what I'm really suppose to do, or if I am so scared to loose my mom that I'm halting any other path because I'm scared if I leave she might not be there when I get back.

And then there's my new father. James is wonderful! Honestly, he is even more than I could hope for and his fiance is so kind and we already had a relationship before I even knew she was marrying him. I mean she wrote my recommendations for the Ireland program. Finishing grad school at GVSU could be amazing. I mean I love the campus. It's comfortable, familiar. It would give me a chance to get to know James better and I would be only a couple of hours away from my family. But is going back to my undergrad university, where I'm comfortable, a step backward? Would having my kind of, almost, stepmom being my program advisor again be weird? And, will I get what I need out of the program if I'm that comfortable?

Mateo. The path I'm most afraid to even write about. I...I love him. Not in the way I loved Simon or Trevor. I love him in a way I wasn't able to love any other man because he made me feel...safe. And in that safety he made me see myself. He awoke in me something I had never felt before, true understanding. He just knew me in a way that no one else really understood and I understood him. And it kills me to know that he's hurting right now, because I know he loves me. If I do choose him, to go back to Ireland and really give it a try with him, would I be making a huge life decision for a guy, again? Would I be making the same mistake I made with Trevor? And If I stay for my mom, would I be making the same mistake I made with Simon? Which lesson am I supposed to apply? Which path should I choose?

My heart wants one thing but my head wants another and I'm just not really sure what to do. Oh, but Mateo has a girlfriend...that's what Saoirse said. I guess I already made one decision. One mistake.

Chapter 22

To my future self,

After a week of self-reflection, and no closer to a decision on which direction to follow that could potentially affect the rest of my life, I decided I needed a break. A break from thinking about school, and my new family, and my old family, and…Mateo.

I barged in my mom's room, flew a suitcase on her bed and started throwing clothes in.

"What are you doing Leena Marie?" my mom yelled as she started picking clothes up off the floor that I was flinging out of her closet.

"We are going on a girl's trip," I said confidently as I threw her yellow polka dot bikini in her suitcase.

"Oh we are?" she said as a phrase instead of a question.

"Yes, we are going to put our feet in the sand and drink Margaritas."

"I can't. I have things to do."

"No, you don't."

"Well, how are we getting there?" she asked.

"I already talked to dad. We are taking the red truck. He just finished fixing up his old car so we're good."

"Oh, you talked to your dad, did you?" she screamed so my dad, Tony, could hear. She walked over to the suitcase and took the bikini out. "This is just for your dad," she said, "Although, he won't be seeing it anytime soon!" she screamed down the hall.

"Yuck," I responded.

"Hey, when you've been married for as long as your dad and I, you find ways of spicing things up every now and then. It's important," my mom said casually as she grabbed a more conservative tankini out of her first drawer.

"Gross."

My mom shrugged her shoulders as she continued to grab clothes out of her drawers. "So, where are we going?"

"I was thinking Myrtle Beach, South Carolina," I replied, still rummaging through her clothes.

"Oh, I heard it's nice there."

"Ya, I have a little money left over from working at Eloise's shop and the library, and I got a good deal on an oceanfront room."

"How fancy," my mom said as she wrapped a scarf around her neck.

"I'm not sure you'll need that at the beach mom," I said walking out of her closet and moving on to her shoes that lined the wall in a beautiful art display.

"Leena. Come here," she said as she patted the bed motioning me to sit next to her. I climbed up on the bed.

"Mom, I really need to do this. My soul is telling me to," I looked up at her with my hands in prayer position silently begging with my hands.

"Fine! But I'm paying for the food and gas," she said as she put a book on her bed in the suitcase.

"Deal!"

"When are we going?" she asked.

"Now. Your suitcase is all packed."

"Uhm, no. I'm going to repack this to make sure I have everything I need and we'll leave in an hour. Last time you packed my suitcase I had to buy new panties at Walmart because all you packed were my period panties."

"To be fair, that's all that was clean," I said as I left her room.

"Leena!"

"Fine, but make it a quick hour," I said from down the hallway.

"Leena Marie. I will take the hour!" she screamed lovingly.

"Ok, ok," I retorted.

To my future self,

My mom and I arrived at the condo I rented at precisely midnight. It took us exactly thirteen hours with all our stops to get photos and snacks. My mom and I used to take a ton of road trips together. It was our thing. Every state has some cheesy welcome center she likes to get snacks at, and she loves to get her photo next to the state sign. She has an album full of photos, even from the same states. It's a quirky collection, but that's my mom.

When we arrived I was relieved that the condo was actually nice and looked like the photos and wasn't some roach infested, flee-bag motel that had probably witnessed a murder, or other serious crime. As I entered the code into the lock from my booking confirmation I couldn't help but be a bit nervous. But I was met with the smell of citrus and fresh towels. We fell right asleep. It was so nice to wake up to the sun peaking through the window the next day.

"Leena...Sweetie...Are you awake?" my mom said from the condo kitchen. I could smell bacon, grits, and eggs as my stomach began to moan.

I took a big yawn, "Good morning mom," I wrapped a silk robe around my body and walked to the kitchen. "That smells incredible."

"I thought you might be hungry," she said as she moved the bacon around in the pan.

I sat down at the kitchen island and ate a piece of fruit as I poured myself a glass of OJ.

My mom sat across from me bringing up both a plate of eggs, grits, and bacon. She put a big bite of grits in her mouth and said, "So, how did you sleep?"

"Manners mom," I replied.

"What? It's just us."

I laughed and took another gulp of OJ. "Good. The bed was surprisingly nice. I don't typically like sleeping in unfamiliar beds."

"What a mother loves to hear," she replied.

"Funny," I said as I took a bite of bacon.

"How much did you pay for this room? It's super fancy," she asked.

"Oh, actually I got a really incredible deal. It was like two hundred bucks for the weekend. We have until Saturday. It's booked on Sunday. I guess someone canceled and they needed to fill the space," I replied.

"Uhm...their loss," my mom said, continuing to talk while she ate her breakfast. "So, do you want to talk about it?"

I looked at her annoyed.

"Come on, Leena. I love our trips and I love that you've gotten your spontaneity back, but I know you. What's going on?"

"Not now. Please."

"Ok. But we have to talk about it sometime. It's too easy to get stuck when you don't share your struggle. And I can feel something is wrong. Mother's intuition."

I wiped my mouth, "Well, I don't appreciate your mother's intuition ruining my wonderful escape from reality."

My mom smiled, "There she is."

"What?"

"My Leena."

I smiled back, understanding she saw the bigger chunks of me coming back from the shattered pieces they used to be.

Breakfast was so good. My mom has a way with food. Anything she makes tastes incredible. I'm not sure if it's a mother's love, nostalgia, or a missed calling to be a chef, but her food makes you feel things.

After eating way more than I should have, we shimmied our bloated tummies into our bathing suits, and walked down to the beach, which just happened to be right outside of our back patio door. The sun felt great! The sun warmed my skin as the ocean breeze cooled me down making today the perfect day for laying out. We grabbed two chairs that we assumed belonged to the house and sat in the shallow part of the water so that our feet were submerged while the rest of our bodies baked in the sun.

My mother took a deep breath, "This is a perfect day. And those can be hard to come by. So, thanks sweetie."

"Thanks for coming," I said back as I sprayed coconut oil on my skin. I laid back and let the sun heat me up. I enjoyed the silence for about twenty minutes, mustering up the courage to say what I needed to say.

"Mom? Are you awake?" I asked.

"I'm here," she replied.

"I'm ready."

My mom took off her sunglasses and turned towards me.

"I...I feel stuck," I said.

"Stuck?" she questioned with a twinge of pain.

"No, no…I feel like I don't know what to do next. That's all. Not that I don't like living with you and dad. That's not what I meant."

"Oh, well, Leena whatever you decide will work out," she said confidently.

"No, it won't. It hasn't before."

"No, Leena. Everything did work out with every choice you made. Maybe not in the way you envisioned, but every decision you made is now part of you. That's how life forces you to grow."

"I didn't see you for 2 almost 3 years! How is that working out? I lost you. I could lose you again?" I replied, trying to choke down tears.

"Oh, so this is what this trip is about," she turned toward me and grabbed my hands. "Leena, like I said before, you never lost me. Sure, we didn't see each other, but I thought about you everyday. I prayed for you everyday. I wished for you to find happiness. I knew things would work out because I trust you. You are so strong and so courageous and kind. I knew that one day you would come back to us, to your family. And I knew one day you would leave again and that's ok. But whether I'm at home with you, a state away, a country away, or even a lifetime away, I'll always be your mom. It's my deepest commitment and greatest blessing. I'll always be with you and I'll always support you in what you think is best for your happiness. Don't let me hold you back sweetie. I'm by your side, always."

"But what if I leave and when I get back you're gone?" I sputtered, releasing tears that were gathering in my eyes.

"Well, I don't plan on dying anytime soon, but if something should happen then always remember that I love you and that I want you to live a full life filled with love and adventure. Don't let the thought of losing me prevent you from becoming you. If you do that, then I've failed you as a mother and as a friend. Please, love courageously, live boldly, and never be afraid to be you. You are the love of my life and the thought of you putting your life on hold for me crushes me, Leena."

I took a deep breath, "I know what I have to do," and with a big smile I jumped on my mom pushing her and her chair back into the sand, "I love you mom."

"I love you too," she responded, and I knew she meant it.

Chapter 23

To my future self,

I made a decision. I picked my path. I'm going back to Ireland. Not just for Mateo, but for me. I have always loved Ireland. I always saw myself there. The only thing holding me back was myself. And now, I finally feel like I'm ready to start living the path I have chosen for myself. Not the path Simon has chosen, or my family, or Trevor, or my new dad. I have made the choice. I took the leap of faith and I'm really damn proud of myself.

I'll be working at Eloise's shop and living in the little apartment above it. I'm excited to see her and tell her everything that happened when she left my house. Saoirse must be really busy with her program because she hasn't called me back or answered any of my texts. I hope she's ok.

James wants to encourage my writing so he actually paid for my whole trip and gave me a couple of thousand dollars to live off of until I start my writing program again. I told him it was way too generous, but he insisted. He said he had a lot of missed birthdays and Christmases to make up for.

I still can't believe how things have worked out. I feel like my life has become a blockbuster movie and I'm the main character...finally! Whatever happens, at least I'm not a side character in my own life anymore.

Chapter 24

To my future self,

I stood silent for a second, remembering that Michelle had told me something very similar. To let Trevor pass through me, to not let his memory get stuck. "Thanks, you have a good day. I'll be around," I smiled at her and turned around walking down the little dirt path and through the old squeaky gate feeling somehow lighter, somehow different.

The day after I landed I was so jet lagged I slept for a full day. Eloise is so kind. She picked me up from the airport and stocked my apartment with groceries and linens. I was staying in a little apartment above her shop. She is seriously the nicest person I've ever met. She seemed a bit quieter than usual. I'm chalking it up to my jetlag.

But there was something I needed to do today. For once in my life, I felt ready to let him go and with him all the tragedy that our relationship inevitably brought. I took a taxi out to the countryside. As I stepped out I took a deep breath. You can do this. Remember, you get to decide what happens next. I told myself.

I was nervous to see him. To see what he had become. Even though I knew I was safe, the shadow of his life surrounded me, hurting me with imprints of his legacy. But he had no power over me anymore. Not today, not tomorrow, not ever. I'm ready to let him go.

I walked the little dirt path, opened the large rusty gate that squeaked as I slowly entered it and searched the old stones for a familiar name. I finally found the stone. It was tall and white. The grass was fresh and there were dried flowers that covered the base. Someone must love him. Someone must miss him. I read the headstone, "Oisin James ó Conchobhair, Husband of Roisin ó Conchobhair, father of Cara ó Conchobhair." Father? He had a daughter? And why wasn't I listed? Sure, I guess he knew I wasn't his daughter, but he raised me for eight years of my life. I guess he didn't love me that way. A deep pain ran through my body as I frowned, choking down tears. I took a deep breath. You get to decide what happens next. I reminded myself. I allowed myself to feel the pain, and in acknowledgement of it, I was able to let it go.

I reached in my backpack and took out a long cardboard box. As I reached inside, I was reminded of the salesman at The Cliffs of Moher and how he probably didn't realize how big of a step it was for me to see my father's family crest. For the first time, I was about to see it, hoping it would help me understand him, this man who brought me such pain. I knelt down and rolled out the large poster against the soft green grass. I flattened it out with my hands.

The crest looked royal, but I suppose they all did. Like it had come straight out of a King Arthur movie. The crest had two lions holding up a tree with its roots exposed. As I stared at the crest I wondered what it meant or even if that truly mattered to me.

"Hello," a woman said as she tapped my shoulder.

"Hi," I responded as I got up and offered my hand.

She shook my hand politely. She was a tall woman with curly blonde hair and fair skin. She looked to be in her fifties and had a fresh bouquet of flowers in her hands, "Did you know James?" she asked.

For a second I froze, realizing the flowers were for my father's grave, "You mean Oisin?" I asked, "I knew him a longtime ago."

"I see. I haven't heard anyone call him Oisin in a long time. Most people knew him by his middle name James," she knelt down and replaced the old flowers with fresh red roses. "These were his favorite flowers."

I made a face of confusion and quickly shook it away, "I didn't know he liked flowers."

"He didn't. Not much at least. But he grew many bushes around our house. Said it reminded him of his daughter."

"Oh, Cara?" I said remembering the name from the headstone.

"No, Cara is our daughter. I mean his first daughter, Leena."

I took a step back and began to tremble.

"Dear are you ok?" the woman said as she looked at me blankly. "Were you close to James? I know his passing was sudden. Are you ok?"

"I'm Leena," I said softly.

The woman's eyes widened as she gave me a big hug. "It's so great to meet you."

I didn't hug her back.

"I'm sorry. You must have a million questions. Ask me anything you like."

I shook my head.

The woman looked at the crest. "If you want to know about your family. You have some cousins that live just down the road that I'm sure would love to meet you."

"No," I replied in a shallow breath. I didn't want to meet anyone that could resemble him.

"Please, Leena. I would really like to answer your questions."

I looked at her and with my voice shaking, I yelled, "He was horrible. He...did...horrible things. How could you love someone like that?" I quickly covered my mouth. I regretted it as soon as the words slipped out. "I am so sorry. I didn't mean to..."

The woman interrupted me. "You're right. He did horrible things to you and you deserve to be angry. He did horrible things to me when we first met too. But then he stopped drinking, and he got help. It was hard for him, shameful. Especially here, in Ireland where alcohol is everywhere. But he did it and then we had Cara and he was good to her and to me," she said.

Her words sliced through me. He changed for them, but not for me.

"He regretted the things he did to you and the way he treated your mom. But, he loved you Leena. He really did. He loved those roses and he took good care of them. I think it was his way of coping with what he did to you. How he treated you. Roses are your favorite, right?" she asked.

"It's not enough."

"I know. And, he knew that too. That's why he never reached out, that's why you're not on the headstone, that's why you haven't heard from him. He agreed to never contact you or your mother and he respected those wishes, but more than that he didn't feel like he deserved a second chance. He didn't want to bring you any more harm than he already had."

I stood silent.

"His biggest regret in life was hurting you, Leena and I wish that were enough, but I know it's not. My father was a hard man, a mean man. I finally ran off and never came back. The beatings never really heal, they just change into something else. I get it. You're not obligated to forgive him. Don't ever let anyone make you feel like you have to," she said.

I looked at her surprised. We both had been with men far too similar to our fathers, but for her it worked out. James changed, he got better. Maybe he saw that she deserved more than the version of him who cared more about himself and beer than anyone else.

"He was a selfish man and I hope he treated you better. You seem like a nice woman," I knelt down and rolled my poster back up. I handed her the family crest. "Here, I don't need it anymore."

"Are you sure?" The woman asked as she gently took the crest.

"Ya, maybe you can give it to Cara. You are his family. If he changed as much as you said he did, then she is probably missing him a lot right now. Even if he wasn't, fathers have a way of lingering around, don't they?"

"I'll make sure she gets it," she said.

"It was really nice meeting you," I looked at my shoes as I kicked the grass softly. "And, thanks. For telling me about my father."

"Leena, I live just down the street. You are welcome to come by anytime. I know Cara would love to meet you. She'll be twelve next week."

"That's nice of you. But it's ok. I have a family."

The woman looked down as if my words had hurt her.

"But maybe we can be friends. Maybe one day you can meet my stepdad Tony or my biological father James."

"James?"

"I know, a weird coincidence right?" I said, remembering to her, Oisin was James.

"I don't believe in coincidences," she said with a smile. "Thank you for chatting with me Leena. For letting me talk to you about my James."

I smiled as I started to walk away.

"Leena!" the woman yelled.

I turned around.

"Don't let him linger in you. Don't for one minute let him control your happiness. Took me a long time to learn that with my own father."

Chapter 25

To my future self,

Today was going to be the day. I'm going to go talk to Mateo. I know he has a girlfriend, but I would never forgive myself if I didn't tell him how I felt or at least explain why I had been acting so weird. I owed him an explanation…no…I owed myself. So, I finished my hair and did my makeup really nice. I even wore the same lipstick I was wearing the night we met, the same shade from our date in the forest.

As I walked down the stairs I bumped into Eloise.

"Hi, Eloise!"

"Well, don't you look nice," she replied.

"Thank you. I was just heading out. Do you need me to open the store before I leave?"

"Oh, don't worry about that. Today's a big day. The store won't be open until next week."

"Is there a holiday or something?" I asked.

Eloise shut her mouth like she was trying to hold something in. "Dear, I have to tell you something and you can't tell anyone I told you."

"Are you ok, Eloise?" I said, suddenly scared she was sick or something.

"No, no, I'm fine. It's just that today is Conor's wedding."

"Wow! Conor is getting married! That's amazing? I'll have to buy him and his new bride a bottle of wine. Who is he marrying? I thought he was head over heels for Saoirse."

"That's who he's marrying," she said as she squinted her eyes.

Pain shot through my head and traveled down my arms lingering in my fingers. "Saoirse...my Saoirse."

"I'm sorry dear. She didn't want me to tell you."

"Why the hell not?"

"It's complicated. That's all."

"Tell me what's going on Eloise!" I demanded.

"I can't. I'm sorry."

"Well, then I'll just have to ask her myself. Where is the wedding?" I asked.

Eloise pointed to the invitation that was sitting on the shop desk. "I'm sorry, Leena. I really wanted to tell you. I love my grandson but..." Eloise fell silent.

"It's ok. I'll take care of it. I'll see you there ok?"

Eloise walked to the back room and I ran out the front of the shop door. Fumbling my keys trying to find the right one to lock the door. I flagged down a taxi and hopped in the front seat quickly giving them the address. It took me half an hour to get to the wedding location and let me tell you, it felt like an eternity.

I arrived at the village hall to find it decorated in light blush flowers and old lace. It was breathtaking, but not Saoirse which made me feel even more uneasy. Something wasn't right.

I snuck past the family and into the bridal suite where I found Saoirse looking at herself in the mirror. She looked up and saw my reflection.

"I thought you might come," she said as she glided a nude shade of lipstick on her lips.

"You did? Because I just found out that my best friend is getting married less than an hour ago."

"This day isn't about you, Leena."

"Pink blush...twinkly lights...apparently it's not about you either," I replied.

"Leena, you can't say things like that to me! It's my wedding day."

"Exactly, it's your wedding day and you don't want your best girl friend here. And the decor, I mean it's stunning, but it looks straight out of a home decor magazine, which is so not you. To think of it, marriage really isn't you. So what's going on? Spill!"

"No."

"Come on Saoirse. I've been trying to reach you for weeks."

"Yes, but you're just now showing up."

"That's not fair Saoirse. I thought you were busy with your graduate project. You told me you got another year's approval, but were still working on the formula."

"Well, it doesn't matter now. That's all over," she said as she put light blush on her cheeks.

"What do you mean?"

"I couldn't figure it out."

"You don't just give up. That's not you."

"I mean, I tried as hard as I could and I couldn't figure it out."

"Bullshit. You don't give up. What's going on?" I demanded.

Saoirse stood up revealing a large bump.

"Oh. Saoirse, congratulations! That's so exciting!" I jumped on her, giving her a big hug. She didn't smile. I stopped. "Are we not happy? I just assumed since there's a bump you were keeping it?"

"I am," she said.

"Wait. You're pretty far along. Does this mean you were pregnant when you came to visit me in Indiana?"

"Yes, I just didn't know it. I found out when I got back. I went to the clinic thinking I had the flu and well, I didn't."

"Ok, so….Conor's the father I'm assuming…"

"No, Dr. Wiser is the father."

"Your advisor!"

"See the problem?"

"Well, that's a bit taboo in the academic world, but not uncommon."

"No, Leena. He's the grant advisor too. If anyone on the ethics committee found out then my whole project, all the progress I've made, could be all for nothing. They'll pull the plug not only on me, but on my graduate partner. I'm so stupid! What was I thinking? I mean we used protection but I guess that .09% chance was bound to happen to me."

"Saoirse, take a deep breath," I said as I gave her a hug.

"No, Leena. I threw my life away. I could have done so much, been so many different versions of myself and I threw that freedom away. And now I have to marry Conor because…"

"Because why?" I was still a little confused how Conor fit into the picture.

"Because…I can't, Leen,." Saoirse wiped the tears from her eyes. "I have to do this."

"No, you don't. Remember, you get to choose what happens next."

Saoirse looked me in the eyes, "He's blackmailing me Leena. He said he'll tell the committee and if they find out, all the research I did would be for nothing. They'll shut down the project and all the progress we've made on the fabric formula. It will ruin everything and the career of my academic partner. I can't do that to her."

"No," I replied.

Saoirse looked at me confused.

"You deserve better." I walked out the door looking for the groom's room. "Conor? Conor! Where are you?! You spineless little twerp of a man!"

His family looked at me concerned and rushed towards me as if to ask me to leave. I made a dash out a side door and ran to a little shack with a sign that read Groom's Room.

I ran with a slew of family members behind me. I flung open the door, and quickly locked it behind me.

"Leena!" a familiar voice said.

I turned around to find Mateo in a tux looking so handsome it knocked the already sparse breath out of me.

"Mateo..."I said, catching my breath.

"What are you doing here Leena?" Conor asked.

I suddenly remembered why I was standing in the middle of this little cottage.

"Conor, not so great to see you," I yelled.

"Good to see you too. Wow, you know it's my wedding day, Leena," he replied.

"Oh, no it's not."

"That's enough Leena!" Conor said in an annoyed tone.

"You cannot do this to Saoirse. It isn't right," I said sternly.

"What does she mean Conor?" Mateo asked, confused.

Of course Mateo didn't know. He would never stand for something like this. He was too good.

"Your friend Conor here is blackmailing Saoirse into marrying him."

"What?" Mateo said as he jolted his eyes towards Conor.

"Conor isn't the father of Saoirse's baby, it's her advisor's child. She told Conor and instead of supporting Saoirse with whatever she wanted to do with the baby, he blackmailed her. Told her if she didn't marry him then she would let the committee know about her and her advisor which means.."

"Her project would have been shut down...because he is the grant advisor," Mateo said quietly putting the pieces together. "Is this true Conor? Is she right?"

"Well, it was too late for her to have an abortion. And you know us, we're meant to be together. It was just a matter of time anyway, so why not speed up the process? I didn't mean anything by it really. She does love me. And, I'll help her take care of the baby, of course, raise it as my own. It's a win win. Why are you looking at me like that Mateo? You know me. I would never do anything to hurt her," Conor replied.

"How could you?!" Mateo screamed as he punched Conor in the face. "You will not go near Saoirse, you will not touch her, you will not say her name, you won't even think of her or I promise you I will hurt you so bad you will wish for death." He unlocked the door and slammed it open to find her family listening in, "Great! Everyone's here. This is what's going to happen, Saoirse will not be embarrassed or shamed and not a one of you will say anything to the university or other villagers, or so help me I will make sure each and every one of you.."

A tall burly man cut him off, "Stop, Mateo! We understand. We will keep Saoirse's secret, she is like family to us. I'm sorry for my son. I will make sure he gets what's coming to him. He'll never make this mistake again or bother Saoirse. Go check on her. The family will clean up the mess." The man walked into the cottage, "And thank you Leena. I don't know how you found out, but I appreciate you stopping the wedding before an even bigger mistake happened. You are welcome in the village anytime. Saoirse is lucky to have you as a friend. I'm sorry about my son."

As I left the cottage I could hear the man screaming at Conor.

I walked back to the bridal suite as Mateo talked with some of the other men standing around the cottage. I would not want to be Conor...

As I walked into the suite Saoirse stood.

"Everything is taken care of," I said as I hugged her.

"I don't understand..." she said, trembling. This was the first time I've ever seen Saoirse scared.

"It's ok. Take a deep breath. Mateo and Conor's dad are taking care of Conor. He won't be saying anything to anyone. No one will. If you want to keep the baby I'll be right here with you every step of the way. And if not, I'll still be right here with you every step of the way. Because that's what you do for the people you love."

"Leena Estrada, I don't deserve you."

I rubbed her back, "We're sisters. You're not losing me that easily. Come on, I'm sure Eloise is here by now. She can take us home to the apartment and we can eat mint chocolate chip ice-cream and watch stand-up."

We hugged in silence for a few minutes. Saoirse wiped her face with a makeup wipe as I unbuttoned her long white dress.

"The decor is hideous isn't it? I would never!" she looked disgusted.

"I know. I know," I said, mimicking her face.

We gathered up her things and caught Eloise as she drove up. Eloise's face seemed both relieved and concerned, but she was happy to see us and to see Saoirse without a wedding ring on her finger.

Chapter 26

To my future self,

I woke up around noon today bloated from all the ice-cream and cheese Saoirse and I ate the night before. I think we ate through all the groceries Eloise stocked the apartment with. We invited Eloise to stay the night with us but she said she needed to check on Conor. While he did a horrible thing, he was still her grandchild and we understood. If there is anyone who can help someone see the error of their misdoing with compassion, it's Eloise.

Saoirse and I stayed up all night talking. She was so excited to tell me all about the advances in her research. She was so close to finding the formula and, in fact, she was confident that her next formula would work. She explained all the chemical reasons, but I'm no scientist so I honestly didn't understand anything she was saying.

I asked her if she thought about what she wanted to do about the baby before talking to Conor and she told me that she didn't want to keep it. She wasn't sure she wanted to be a mom. Not now, maybe not ever. It was too late to have an abortion, and even if she could, she wasn't sure she had the strength to do it. Her plan was to have the baby and give it up for adoption. She said that when Conor heard her say that something in him must have snapped. He always envisioned having a family with her and knowing that she wasn't open to being a mom caused him to do things she didn't even know he was capable of. He's not allowed to have a dream with her though, not if it's not something she wants. Honestly, it's creepy just thinking about it. Saoirse said his mom died a couple of years ago and ever since he's been a little off. She's hoping he'll go to counseling and get help. He is one of her oldest friends. He's seen every version of her and Saoirse isn't ready to end the friendship if he's willing to go to counseling and get help. She's kind but I'll make sure I'm by her side, not only with her pregnancy, but to help keep those safe boundaries so Conor can't hurt her again. Second chances are a gift, not an obligation, and I'll make sure he understands that.

I told her that her adoption plan is a beautiful idea. I shared that my stepfather adopted me and that I know it's not exactly the same, but that he was the best dad I could have asked for. She said that reflecting on my mom's story really gave her the strength to make the decision. There was so much she wanted in life not only for her but for her baby and she wanted them both to have the best life and opportunities available. We're going to an adoption agency next week to learn more about the process.

She apologized for ignoring me, explaining that she didn't want to put one more thing on me because of everything I had been through. I reminded her that our friendship is interdependent. We help each other no matter what not because we need to, but because we choose to. That's what friendship is all about; choosing to show up for each other.

After facemasks Saoirse fell asleep on the couch and didn't wake up until about five that evening. "Good morning!" she said as she walked into the kitchen.

I served her a big plate of spaghetti, "You mean good evening," I said.

"Wow, I did not mean to sleep that late. I'm just so tired all the time."

"That would be the baby," I reminded her.

"Right," she said, taking a big bite of spaghetti. We sat and ate for about an hour chatting. It felt nice to feel normal.

"So, how was it seeing Mateo?" she asked as she took a big gulp of water.

"Well, I was taken off-guard and I didn't really get to say much to him. I...it wasn't what I had planned."

"Oh, you had something planned did you?" Saoirse said with raised eyebrows.

"Look, I know he has a girlfriend but I just..."

Saoirse cut me off, "Love him."

I shook my head yes.

"Well, good because he loves you and he doesn't have a girlfriend."

"What?" I replied in shock.

"I'm sorry! He was heartbroken and I thought you were over him so I told you he had a girlfriend so you wouldn't contact him and let him move on. You are my girl but he is like my brother. It's just how it is."

"Saoirse, how could you?"

"I'm sorry, I'm sorry. But look I tried to set him up a couple of times and he wouldn't have any of it. Not even a one night stand. He's really into you, Leena. I mean he doesn't even look at any other girls and you guys aren't even together. It's crazy. I don't understand. But then again I've never been.."

"In love?" I asked.

Saoirse shook her head. "Let me make it up to you. He's playing tonight at The Kings Head, the show starts at 7. If you leave now you might catch him before he goes on stage."

"I can't see him like this!" I motioned to my body which was wearing sweatpants and a baggy shirt with spaghetti stain decor.

"Ok, we can do this! Get it together Leena! Go do your makeup and I'll go and find you an outfit," Saoirse stood, "Break!" she said as she clapped her hands and walked to the bedroom.

I stood outside of The Kings Head too nervous to move forward. Saoirse had outdid herself. She dug out the same outfit I wore the night I first met Mateo. My tight maroon dress with puffed sleeves and buttons down the back. My big curls tightened away from my face with the black scarf Eloise gave me and my mom's deep red lipstick painted on my nervous lips. My tribe was with me and I needed their courage.

I could hear the music from the bar, Mateo must have already started his set. I took a deep breath and walked in gracefully in my high heels. The bar was alive with dancing and singing. I maneuvered through the crowd and went over to the bar. I gestured to the bartender and said, "I'll have a jack and coke, and I think maybe you should buy me this one, what do you say?" The bartender smiled as he nodded his head and handed me the drink.

I went to the back of the pub trying to find a clearing. And then Mateo stopped singing. I turned around worried something had happened to him. Our eyes locked. "Leena!?" He yelled over the mic. "Leena, is that you?"

I felt naked as everyone in the pub stared at me. I mouthed, hi, and, I'm sorry.

"Ok, everyone make a path for my dear Leena in the back," he said into the mic.

The crowd parted as jealous girls were, once again, murdering me with their eyes. I walked down the path until I reached the stage. Mateo grabbed me, pulling me up onto the stage.

"Mateo, I..." he pulled me in, hugging me close. "I love you, and I'm sorry." I whispered into his ear.

"I love you too." He whispered back. He grabbed my face staring deeply into my eyes. I could feel his gaze in my soul, in my body. It felt like for the first time I was letting him truly see me, all of me. In that moment, I peeled back all the hidden layers, giving him my bare soul in front of everyone in the pub. He leaned in and kissed me. A rush of excitement traveled through my body lingering in my fingers. I pulled him in tighter as we embraced, the crowd cheering in the background.

After a few seconds Mateo pulled away and smiled, "I've been waiting to do that for some time now." He turned to the crowd directing his attention to the mic, "So, this is my girlfriend Leena. She just moved here...wait, did you move back?" he asked me.

I shook my head yes.

"I should know these things. I am her boyfriend...I'm your boyfriend, right?"

I shook my head yes again, not able to get the school girl smile off my face.

"Great, glad we agree. It would have been really awkward if you said no."

The crowd laughed. He really knew how to command an audience.

"Anyway, my girlfriend here just moved back to Ireland from America and she happens to be the best Britney Spears impersonator, so boys what do you think?" he looked back at his band. "Should I play Leena's song?" he asked the crowd.

Oh shit! Oh shit! He wasn't! He was...! I told myself mouthing no at him.

He turned to the band and they all shook their heads in agreement as they started to play Toxic by Britney Spears.

"Come on love, you know you want to," he said as he motioned me closer.

He was so cute, how could I say no? I took the mic and became Britney once again at the Irish pub I reluctantly went into one night many nights ago. The Leena standing here tonight was much different than the Leena that walked in begrudgingly, not knowing that the night would be a catalyst for healing and a path for love.

But the soul wants what the soul wants. For the first time my path felt clear and I felt like I finally had a story to tell and a life to live.

Sincerely,

Leena Estrada

Epilogue

My Little Love,

I didn't know if I could be your momma, but I'm so glad that I am. I fell in love with you long before you were even conceived. Growing up, I wasn't sure if I wanted to be a mom, but now I know you were a dream I was afraid to dream and that my heart always belonged to you. You have given me a purpose I didn't know I was capable of. You were love at first sight and I am so happy that I get to be your momma. It's a special thing, the relationship between mother and daughter and I can't wait to get to know you.

Love,

Your Momma

-Excerpt from the next book in the series, Tiger Among Lilies.

Letter from the Author

Honestly, I never thought I would be here sharing my writing with others. It's been a lifelong dream of mine that I was too afraid to reach for. For years I struggled with the feelings of not being enough, birthed from trauma. As part of my healing journey I began to write again, a passion I used as a child to get through hard times, and something I left behind when I ran from my past. At first it was a struggle to write. For about a year I started stories that lacked authenticity and because of that I never finished them. I didn't feel connected to them. I was afraid to share myself, my story. Through therapy and beautiful relationships, I began to pick up the pieces of my shattered self-worth. I began confronting my past and healing for the first time in my adult life. Through that healing this story poured out of me. I wrote it in just a few months. This is a work of fiction, but many of the events are based on my personal experiences and feelings during those times. Writing this story is my mark of healing, and I hope that in sharing this story, other women find courage and hope in their healing journey. After all, we are a tribe of roses.

   -K Stikeleather